I WILL NOT DO THIS. . . .

I pressed my hand to my wrist but instead of pushing the wires of the remote together, I pulled the knot that unbound the bomb strapped to my leg. I was supposed to do this to make sure the bomb did not have to explode through me. It slithered down, sliding on my sweat-drenched skin, and landed by my foot.

My skirts belled over it, but I still didn't push the wires. Instead, I nudged the bomb under a banner hanging in front of me, Keran Berj's smile, printed bigger than the tallest man, watching my face.

I took a step back. Three little girls walked onstage. There were flowers in their hands. The Minister of Culture smiled.

People laughed, happy at the sight.

I knew something was truly wrong with me then. I was where I was supposed to be. I was doing everything I was supposed to do.

Only I wasn't.

I kept moving, let myself be pushed far back into the crowd, let myself be carried to its very edge by those who wanted to be closer. Who wanted to see the old, tired man onstage.

Who believed in what they were seeing.

Then I pressed the wires together.

OTHER BOOKS YOU MAY ENJOY

After	Amy Efaw
Battle Dress	Amy Efaw
Extraordinary	Nancy Werlin
Fire	Kristin Cashore
The Grimm Legacy	Polly Shulman
Impossible	Nancy Werlin
Matched	Ally Condie
Nightshade	Andrea Cremer
Sunshine	Robin McKinley
XVI	Julia Karr

elizabeth scott

GRACE

speak
An Imprint of Penguin Group (USA) Inc.

Speak
Published by the Penguin Group
Penguin Group (USA) Inc., 345 Hudson Street, New York, New York 10014, U.S.A.
Penguin Group (Canada), 90 Eglinton Avenue East, Suite 700, Toronto, Ontario, Canada M4P 2Y3
(a division of Pearson Penguin Canada Inc.)
Penguin Books Ltd, 80 Strand, London WC2R 0RL, England
Penguin Ireland, 25 St Stephen's Green, Dublin 2, Ireland (a division of Penguin Books Ltd)
Penguin Group (Australia), 250 Camberwell Road, Camberwell, Victoria 3124, Australia
(a division of Pearson Australia Group Pty Ltd)
Penguin Books India Pvt Ltd, 11 Community Centre,
Panchsheel Park, New Delhi - 110 017, India
Penguin Group (NZ), 67 Apollo Drive, Rosedale, Auckland 0632, New Zealand
(a division of Pearson New Zealand Ltd)
Penguin Books (South Africa) (Pty) Ltd, 24 Sturdee Avenue,
Rosebank, Johannesburg 2196, South Africa

Registered Offices: Penguin Books Ltd, 80 Strand, London WC2R 0RL, England

First published in the United States of America by Dutton Books,
a member of Penguin Group (USA) Inc., 2010
Published by Speak, an imprint of Penguin Group (USA) Inc., 2011

1 3 5 7 9 10 8 6 4 2

THE LIBRARY OF CONGRESS HAS CATALOGED THE DUTTON BOOKS EDITION AS FOLLOWS:
Scott, Elizabeth, date.
Grace / Elizabeth Scott.—1st ed. p. cm.
Summary: Sixteen-year-old Grace travels on a decrepit train toward a border that may not exist,
recalling events that brought her to choose life over being a suicide bomber, and dreaming of
freedom from the extremist religion-based government of Keran Berj.
ISBN: 978-0-525-42206-8 (hardcover)
[1. Fantasy. 2. Despotism—Fiction. 3. Insurgency—Fiction. 4. Fugitives from justice—Fiction.]
I. Title.
Pz7.S4195Gr 2010 [Fic]—dc22 2009053285

Speak ISBN 978-0-14-241975-5

Designed by Abby Kuperstock
Set in Bel MT Regular

Printed in the United States of America

You're crazy. You fall down,   stand up and walk again,

your ankles and your knees move

but you start again   as if you had wings.

The ditch calls you, but it's no use   you're afraid to stay,

and if someone asks you why,   maybe you turn around and say

that a woman and a sane death   a better death wait for you.

—FROM *Forced March* BY MIKLÓS RADNÓTI

GRACE

CHAPTER 1

I'm afraid my hair is showing. Chris said the dye would work but I'm not sure he much cared if it did; and I don't think it was true dye, just a mixture of color he'd created, a kind of a paint and nothing more. Plus the train is hot, so hot the floor burns my feet, little red huff hisses of pain searing up into my legs.

I want to get off this train but I can't. Not now. It is the only choice left to me, and it is actually considered an honor to be here. To be trusted enough to be on this train, to have a ticket for it, is something most can't even dare to dream of. Keran Berj lets few people out of this land—his land, or so he says—and only those on government business are allowed to go. And then only if the business will result in glory of some kind for Keran Berj.

I'm certainly not supposed to have the honor of being on this train.

I'm not supposed to be here at all.

Chris made my hair glow over a sink, frowning when I tried to move away from the scissors in his hand. The gold I'd given him to help me had bought me no trust and only a tiny bit of his patience.

So now I worry that the bright color is bleeding, raining off my hair and onto my skin. Stupidly, I worry that it is staining my shirt. It is white, with buttons made of tin. One of the sleeves has been sewn in crooked, a large gathered fold lying where my shoulder is.

I've never had a shirt made by machines before.

Inside the fold is space for three of my fingers, like a hiding place in the open, an error made by the machine that sewed the shirt. I was fascinated by it for a while, slipped my fingers into it when we first got on the train until Kerr, the boy Chris made me wait for, the one who I must pretend is my brother, kicked me in the ankle, hard, and hissed, "Stop acting like a piece of Hill shit," as he pretended to be checking the lumpy, stained seat waiting for us.

It's an insult here, in this world. In Keran Berj's world. To be from the Hills is an insult. I hate that, even as I know I would never go back there.

Can't go back there.

Once this train was very grand, or so the stories go. Before Keran Berj, who supposedly rules us all, there was someone else, someone who truly did command everyone's loyalty, a great man who ruled from far away. He is said to have had the strength of a bear and the wisdom of the Saints. He came only once a year to take money and did not crack the dead's teeth to pull out their fillings and melt them into statues. This man came and rode everywhere—from the mountains to the seas— in a long, beautiful train. Its insides were covered with diamonds, and at night it shone brighter than the stars.

Then the man died. No one else came to rule— we were forgotten—and Keran Berj stepped forward and said he would lead, that everyone would be equals and life would be better.

I wonder if it is a rule that all stories must end with a lie. But then, the only stories I know are the ones the People tell, and they all end with Keran Berj and his false words, so maybe there are some that don't.

It is so hot. My hair is wet when I push my fingers into it, my feet hurt, and the man in front of us smells like onions, the wild ones that grow on the side of the Hills. The ones you can smell before you see them, the ones that start to grow with the promise of spring. I can hardly believe this train was grand once, but I see hints of it in the markings where things have been pried away, decorations and comforts removed for someone else's use.

Keran Berj's use. No one will mention this, though. The train is—and will always be—called glorious in spite of its sad state, because not only do you never know who is watching, you never know who is listening. Even those trusted enough to have tickets for this train, this trip, watch what they do. What they say. The train is special, and so is everyone on it, but no one is above Keran Berj.

No one.

At least, according to him.

"Are you asleep, sister?" Kerr asks, and puts his hand on my elbow, stilling my fingers as they twist through my damp hair.

"No," I say, and lower my hand, place it in my

lap on top of my fake papers. There is no stain on my fingers. The dye holds. When I am safely across the border, the first thing I will do is leave Kerr behind.

I would kill him, but I already know I am too weak for that.

CHAPTER 2

*T*he People don't do that," I'd said when Chris told me to take my hair down, and he'd looked at me as if I were stupid, as if he was thinking about tossing me out onto the street right then.

He didn't do that, though. He just frowned at me—like he was weighing his options, weighing my worth—and then yanked my braids down. I'd looped them up so they lay on the back of my neck, and it was still strange to feel air rushing over them after so many years of a sun-crisp cap cradling my skin.

The People believe a woman's hair should be covered, undone only in private. There are exceptions, of course. I was one once.

Chris burned the braids after he cut them off. I stared into the bowl of the sink, at cracked white showing rust underneath. My head burned from the dye he'd concocted. My eyes watered from it. My braids made a peculiar crackling noise as they burned, and smelled terrible too, like a bad dream I couldn't—or wouldn't—remember.

"If it was last year, I'd sell them," Chris said. "Keran Berj wanted women to have shoulder-length hair then. Now it's supposed to be short— new rule—but until recently people were cutting open graves in the hopes of finding hair to add to their own. Imagine walking around with hair smelling of death swinging in your face. But still, better than you swinging from a rope, right?"

I closed my eyes and tried not to think about

how much my scalp hurt. Tried not to think about graves and hanging.

But then, death has always followed me.

"You didn't think to cut your hair before you came here?" he asked as water, so cold there were tiny bits of ice in it, poured out of the tap and over my skull.

"No," I said, and watched the color that was supposed to sink into my hair race in rivers toward the drain. "Will this color hold?"

"It's dye, isn't it?" he said, and yanked a hunk of hair on the back of my neck, pulling me up like the Rorys do to the boys when they first fall off their horses. In the sliver of mirror he'd nailed to the wall, my face was red dark from the blood pulsing into it as I'd knelt over the sink, a color I used to wish I was, but my hair barely touched my ears and shone bright like the sun.

CHAPTER 3

The heat makes me sleepy, but I don't want to sleep. The few times I have, I've drifted off into strange, unpleasant dreams. Awake, I can keep them away and keep an eye on the train. On Kerr.

I close my eyes anyway because I'm tired, end-lessly tired, and the heat makes it worse, and when I look over at Kerr, I don't see him.

Instead, I see Liam.

Liam is now sitting next to me, grim-faced like

always and smacking the heel of one hand against his other palm, a coil of wires—blue, red, yellow, and green—around his wrists.

I wake up with a start just as Liam pushes them together, and the dream clouds my mind as the train groans like Liam's Ma did when her joints were aching and she wanted me to rub them, a long, slow screech that made my teeth ache with wanting to scream.

But if I didn't scream while kneading Liam's Ma's feet, Liam frowning disappointed at me and treating our being pledged as if it was a chore he had to grit his teeth and get through, I won't scream now.

Instead I look at the doors.

They are at either end of the train car, a way out that's useless. The ground we cover now is turning to desert, to bleak, endless bright sand.

The doors are heavy, tarnished metal, and slide open if you press a palm against them. I've never seen anything so fancy. No one opens them except the soldiers. If you want food, you go to the door and wait for a soldier to come through, then follow behind. You have to do the same thing for the washroom, and I think of how Chris used to only let me out twice a day, of how I'd race to the washroom with hate burning a hole in my heart each time.

Maybe he was getting me ready for this, but I don't think he was.

I think I fit into his plans and so he took me in.

Past that, I think he simply didn't care.

CHAPTER 4

*O*nce, right before Mary was sent on her way, I walked down to the main camp, past all the Rorys resting before their next fight, to see Da. I only did it to show things were different for me. Mary had no family that counted to see her before she left, but I did, didn't I? She was alone, aside from her beaten down mother, and I wasn't. I wasn't like her. She was so eager to please and I was . . .

I was where I had to be.

I found Da asleep on the ground near where he'd set up, stinking of drink like always. I slept out under the stars, knowing better than to go into Da's tent without permission. Even then, when Da woke and got a glimpse of me, he smacked me hard.

"Angel House turned you out?" he said, and turned away from me, spat on the ground three times.

"No," I said, and wondered why I'd even come to see him.

"Good. Working for the People's freedom, you are. Proof you're good for something." He waved me away then, and spit three times again as I left.

I nodded even though he couldn't—didn't—see. Even though the People's freedom didn't seem to think much of me. It turned me into a thing. A weapon.

It felt like a cage, being what I was. I felt like I—Grace—was nothing.

I seemed to be the only one who felt that way, though. Lily and Ann loved saying they were Angels and longed for their pledges and bombs like nothing else. Mary never talked about pledging, but then no one would have her since not one of the Rorys was willing to claim her—and the half of her that flowed with the blood of the People— as his.

She did talk about her bomb, though. She wanted it so badly, and when she finally got it, she spent days oiling it so it would slide down her leg without a sound.

No one would go near her because she wasn't one of the People. She was alive only because she was an Angel—and she was glad of it. Glad to be an Angel because then she thought she mattered.

I never understood that. She didn't. I didn't. No Angel did, not truly.

"Stop staring, sister," Kerr says, low-voiced, and I look at him. He's staring out the window, as if the view is going to change. I wonder if he's ever seen the desert before and bet he hasn't, not even in pictures.

If he was in the Hills he'd stare so much he'd fall right off them.

"Don't look at me either," he says, still whispering. As if the snoring people around us are awake and watching. The heat has slowed everything down, made everything an effort. We've only had our papers checked once in the last four stops, so different from the beginning, when the air in the City turned my breath to ghost white puffs and I sat in the train station, waiting.

Then, everyone's papers were checked constantly, and I waited for Kerr, holding his set and fearing they'd be found. My heart hammered so hard I wondered if it was going to break.

"You look sickly," I tell Kerr, and he does. He's so pale I suspect he'd cook in the Hills. Not that he'd ever even make it to them. His throat would be slit by the Rorys before he made it onto the first

slopes. The look of him—no earth color at all—
gives him away right off.

"I'm—" Kerr says, fiddling with the collar on
his shirt, and the door at the far end of the car
opens, soldiers streaming in.

"Papers!" they bark, and then say it again, louder, because they've been drinking—I can smell it—
and because they're bored.

And, I think, because when the train finally
stops and lets everyone on board out to go and do
the government work Keran Berj wants them to
do, they have to ride all the way back to the City.
To him. Not that they would ever let themselves
think this. Not when they have the majesty that is
Keran Berj watching them.

The heart is a place with worm holes made by
feelings you aren't supposed to have but do. I know
that better than anyone.

I get my papers out and put them in my right
hand. Chris told me Keran Berj made it illegal to
gesture with your left hand in honor of the Min-

ister of Culture, who'd lost his left hand due to infection.

"Or Keran cutting it off, most likely," Chris said, laughing, and I smiled and swallowed hard around the bits of bread and meat he'd given me to eat, willing them back down my throat.

I never knew if Chris guessed exactly what I'd done, and I surely wasn't going to ask. It was bad enough to be locked in that room of his house and hear him coming and going, hear people on the street calling him "Christaphor"—his given name, I suspect, or at least the one he'd chosen to use— with respect in their voices, the kind of respect that only comes from fear.

I was afraid of him too.

The soldiers come down the train aisle, plucking up papers and tossing them back. Sometimes they stop and frown and ask questions. Kerr and I have only had to tell our story twice, but now I wonder if we will have to say it again.

We're on our way to bring our sister home. She wants to come back to Keran Berj, to her children and her husband, but the government across the border—never say its name, never acknowledge that it has any power—says she's an escapee. As if anyone traveling outside would ever want to leave the glory that is Keran Berj.

Still, she can't leave unless family comes to claim her, and with her husband off doing his annual soldier training—God watch over him—Kerr was sent instead, and had to bring me because she's pregnant, heavily so, and everyone knows what Keran Berj says about women and childbirth. "Glorious work, fit only for our sisters." Even over the border, his reach extends, proclaiming that only women should be present when babies are born.

As if Keran Berj does not take those children and teach them to act according to his will as soon as he can.

A soldier, blond hair and jagged teeth, stops by

our seats. He flips through my papers and tosses them back. He goes through Kerr's more slowly, then slaps them against one thigh and says, "You look familiar. Did you go to the Academy?"

"I work near it," Kerr says. "Keran Berj Shoes, over on Berj One Road. You've been there, I suppose?"

The soldier nods. "Last year. I waited in line for a whole day, and then the Official for Distribution came and said they ran out."

"Next time you get selected for a pair, tell the Line Officer that Kerr asked you to ask about his nephew's birthday," Kerr says, and the soldier grins. His face is like the moon, wide and waxy-white.

"I hear there's a drawing coming during the Festival of Health."

Kerr nods, and the soldier hands him his papers back before moving on. I finger my hair again as I test the floor with one foot.

Still too hot to rest against.

Still no stain on my hands.

It's a strange road that's led me here. A bad one, some would say. Evil, even. But I'm not sorry I'm here.

I'm not sorry I'm alive.

CHAPTER 5

I was supposed to die before I turned seventeen. I was supposed to drift up into the sky, into the arms of the Saints.

I was an Angel, and I was supposed to honor the People. I was supposed to show that we won't be bent to Keran Berj's will, that we have resources beyond the Rorys.

Keran Berj has his soldiers to make up his army,

the one that enforces his rules, and his Guard, to strike when he needs death to be a sure thing; but he does not have what the People do.

The Rorys fight, and that is all they do. It is their life. They fight to keep the Hills ours, and are named, of course, for Rory. The first one, the one who walked down from the Hills when Keran Berj was young and promising so much it was obvious—at least to the People—that he was a liar.

Rory knew that Keran Berj wanted to control everything. He saw that Keran Berj had no respect for the land, for the Saints, for anything or anyone but himself and his God, and so he walked down from the Hills and went to the City.

He found Keran Berj walking through the City, back before he had so much power he only had to show pictures of his face to be obeyed, and Rory shot him.

He missed, and Keran Berj turned his newly formed Guard on him.

Rory was hung after they were through with him.

Just before he swung, Rory cried out, "You aren't forever, Keran Berj, but the land is. I die for it gladly."

There were still newspapers then, not just the one that Keran Berj controls now, and those words were printed. What Rory said reached back to the People, and they understood what needed to be done. They understood that Keran Berj would not be stopped by anyone but them.

They saw he would want the Hills.

And so the Rorys were born, and now that is what every boy is trained to be. What every man does until he has sons of his own who can go out and fight.

The People are the Hills. The Hills are the People. The Rorys fight to keep what should be as it is, and to remind Keran Berj that he is not forever.

Only the land is.

But there are more than the Rorys. The People have Angels too. They are reminders, in form and action, that Keran Berj will understand, that he cannot—will not—control the People. That we choose as we will.

Keran Berj has posters of Angels in the soldiers' and guards' training camps, we were told as we were training, pictures of red-earth women with bared teeth and wings dripping blood growing out of their backs.

No wonder so few of us are ever even noticed before we do what we are meant to do. If we could arrive on wings and draw blood without blowing it out of people, I think Keran Berj might step aside. His God speaks to him, or so he says, but his God doesn't grant miracles like that.

Of course, the Saints don't either. I know. I had no wings that could help me fly away. To get away from the bomb that was made for me. That was my life.

Sometimes, I don't think there is anything beyond what is here, what is now. I think that maybe
beyond this world—this train, this desert we are
passing through, this heat swelling all around—
there is nothing.

CHAPTER 6

I was supposed to kill the Minister of Culture. I was supposed to stand in the front row of those gathered to listen to him speak and press my left hand to my right wrist in a way that would push the wires bound under my sleeve together.

I was supposed to do that and then watch the world burn.

I wouldn't see it for long. An Angel's death is

quick and painless. Beautiful, like going to sleep on a warm spring night.

Of course, there were no Angels to ask about it. None of them ever came back. They went to the Saints, to beyond. All I heard were stories.

And then there were the burns Ann, Mary, Lily, and I got as we were learning to make bombs, to use them. The way we sometimes singed our hair and how Lily once managed to lose one of her toes—

Those moments were not without pain.

To this day, I can still see Lily's face, gray with agony, and the way her toe lay there on the ground, pulsing blood like it was still part of her. Like it was still living.

It's nothing, we were told. You belong to the Saints. You are their instrument. You will make us proud.

Lily's toe was swept away because it didn't matter. She learned to walk well enough without it. She would be able to do what she was made for.

She would still be able to die.

CHAPTER 7

I was given to Liam two months before I was
sent to the Minister of Culture. Angels are lucky
because they do not have to wait until they are
twenty to be pledged, as other girls do. They do
not have to scurry behind the Rorys carrying
weapons and supplies. They do not have to learn
to live life on the move.

I lived in the sturdy, stone Angel House. I
learned how to talk like someone who lived for

Keran Berj. I learned every rule he decreed, and kept track of the ones he still believed in, as well as the former ones he'd deemed evil. I learned his life story, like all those who follow him do, and what prayers he'd written to have sung to his God. I learned how I would destroy part of his world. And when I was sixteen and four months, I was pledged.

The best Angels die pregnant. There is no sure way to tell before they go, of course, because Angels are only pledged long enough for there to be the chance of a baby and nothing more, but there is always hope sent along. If there is a speck in the body, the marker of another life, then two of the People have died, and it proves that the People value the land and its call above all else.

Keran Berj says this is inhuman, but then Keran Berj hanged his own son for "evil thoughts."

I did not worry that I was carrying a child. Liam came to me only a handful of times, and when he did, he always spoke of Sian and how he was waiting for her.

He always said her name.

I knew how it would be as soon as I saw him; Da's hand on his shoulder, as if to make sure he stayed, and Liam's weary, displeased face as I lifted my face to see him.

It never occurred to him that I didn't want him either. He never questioned the tea I drank every morning, one made of things that shouldn't be named. One that women with many children used when they were desperate to bear no more.

Liam never asked me anything.

CHAPTER 8

I couldn't do it, though.

That was the thing, in the end.

I couldn't die.

I went into the village. I was pale enough, from my bad blood and being sheltered in the Angel House, and dressed properly, my hair painted with lemon water to hide the red that lurked inside its too-light-for-the-People shade and put up, braided and wrapped around my head like the Rorys had seen girls in the village wearing when they were scouting it. I looked like a child of Keran Berj's followers, I looked like every other girl there. Pale faced, light-haired, dressed in swirling white and a shawl with Keran Berj's face printed on it draped over my shoulders and dipping across my back, so that his profile was everywhere you looked.

I stood near the stage, feeling the wind blow through my hair, a strange sensation. I watched and listened as Keran Berj's latest missives from his God were issued. All doctors had to pray to Keran Berj before they saw patients. All corn that was planted had to be the yellow-seeded kind. No one was allowed to go swimming. The Festival of Service was now The Festival of Glorious Freedom.

Money was to be sent to Keran Berj for a palace made of ice that would sit in the desert, a building that would be put under a dome to show that, with Keran Berj, all things were possible.

I bowed my head when the speech ended with "As God wills," as I had been taught.

When I looked up, the Minister was coming onstage. He walked slowly, and was sweating. I felt hot myself, inside the layers of white, under the weight of the shawl. My head felt hot and naked.

I moved my hand to my wrist. I glanced up at the sky. I waited to feel the Saints with me.

I felt nothing.

I pressed my hand to my wrist but instead of pushing the wires of the remote together, I pulled the knot that unbound the bomb strapped to my leg. I was supposed to do this to make sure the bomb did not have to explode through me. It slithered down, sliding on my sweat-drenched skin, and landed by my foot.

My skirts belled over it, but I still didn't push the wires. Instead, I nudged the bomb under a banner hanging in front of me, Keran Berj's smile, printed bigger than the tallest man, watching my face.

I took a step back. Three little girls walked onstage. There were flowers in their hands. The Minister of Culture smiled. One of the girls waved at someone in the crowd, flowers dancing in her hand with the movement.

People laughed, happy at the sight.

I took another step back.

I knew something was truly wrong with me then. I was where I was supposed to be. I was doing everything I was supposed to do.

Only I wasn't.

I kept moving, let myself be pushed far back into the crowd, let myself be carried to its very edge by those who wanted to be closer. Who wanted to see the old, tired man onstage.

Who believed in what they were seeing.

Then I pressed the wires together.

CHAPTER 9

The blast would have killed me had I stayed with the bomb by the stage. I would have been tossed up into the air as bits of bone and ash so fine I would have fallen like rain, scattered like the words of a prayer.

Instead, I stayed standing. Breathing.

Whole.

I can still see the fire the bomb created. It was

so strong, so angry. It hissed and popped and roared as it moved. As it grew.

I walked out of the village, past dazed and weeping women, men, children, and soldiers, slipping into the trees, up into the Hills. I unbraided my hair as I walked, tucking it away under the cap I'd kept in my skirt's waistband, another thing that was to be found on my dead body, another reminder of who and what I was.

Those who had brought me, who hid and watched from far off, to view my destruction—they had horses. They were gone by the time I reached where they'd been, and they'd left no trail, only a tiny patch of trampled grass. It didn't matter. I still knew the way.

My walk was long, but eventually I reached the path that led to where we were living until the winter. It was then I saw the stuffed white sack hanging from a tree.

I stopped and watched it swing.

I had only ever seen one once before, when Sean Cuclani was found down off the Hills inside a house with a soldier. Some say Sean was spying for Keran, others that he'd turned away from the People and that the reason his wife never swelled with child was because he wouldn't touch her.

Either way, the white sack was hung, his things stuffed inside and cursed with all the vengeance the Saints can bring. It was left for him to find. Left for him to see that he had no one. Not the Hills. Not the People. He was nothing. Forgotten. Worse than a ghost, because no one would honor his spirit. No one would ever even say his name again.

Sean took down the sack and hanged himself with the rope. He was left for the earth to take, of course—it wasn't right to bury him, not even then—but he did the proper thing. The honorable thing.

I took down the sack and didn't even think

about the rope. My dead body, whole with my tongue hanging from my mouth, would mean nothing. Likely as not, no one but the birds would ever see it as the People would be on the move soon enough now that I wasn't dead—Keran Berj would send his Guards out looking as soon as he got word—and the birds would just pick me clean without ever wondering why I was there.

I took my good shoes, the sturdy, handmade ones I wore every day, from inside the sack, and then went to find Liam, rope in hand. I don't know what I thought I was going to do.

It doesn't matter anyway. Liam was dead when I got there, laid out in his mother's tent, waiting for respects to come. There was a cloth over his belly, to show he'd stabbed himself in shame over me.

If I was dead, he'd be alive. He'd be celebrating. He'd probably even get Sian, finally.

I took the belt lying around his hips, heavy gold shaped in a pattern of running horses. His

Ma saw me and didn't even spit three times before she started screaming curses.

I ran then, and didn't look back. I didn't stop to see if Da was alive, or if what I'd done had made him do the proper thing and stab himself too.

I'm his daughter, and I'm sure he's still alive.

Strangest thing about all of it is that I think of the village. A place not even in the Hills, and I wonder if the Organizer for Events was killed for having an Angel come. I wonder if Keran Berj sent his cameras to take pictures of the fire's aftermath. I wonder what happened to the flowers that had been so bright onstage. I'd seen them as I left, their color washed away. I wondered if Keran Berj would find them and put them on a poster, would use them as a sign of the People's evil.

I knew the People would use them if they found them too, take the image to heart and leave blood-drenched flowers behind on soil Keran Berj destroyed by overfarming, show that he killed the land, that he cared for nothing but his own will.

I hope the flowers wilted into nothing before anyone found them. They were true flowers once, but then they were picked from the earth and pressed into hands.

They were dead long before I reached them.

CHAPTER 10

Sometimes when I dream, I am lying on that stage, unable to move.

I am lying on the stage, and I watch blood come toward me. I feel it come into me, feel it become me until it is all I am, until it is all I breathe, until I am swallowed by it.

The worst part isn't that I can't stop it. The worst part is that I already know blood won't change anything.

CHAPTER 11

*O*nce Lily told me she'd heard that long ago, back before anyone ruled, back when the People weren't the only ones living in the Hills, others used to worship in the Angel House. She said they prayed to their gods where we practiced making bombs.

"Other gods? Not the Saints?" I said, and she nodded, pointing at the ceiling, and said that was surely why they were no longer in the Hills.

I'd wondered about that over the years, though.

We'd been told the building had been made by the Saints, but as I grew to know the place, and the carvings high on the walls, I decided—

I decided that was wrong.

The carvings were like nothing any Saint ever called for. They were strange, tiny stone faces like monsters out of a dream, and they perched high up on the wall with stone angel wings carved into their backs. Fierce, like they were guarding something. As if they were watching us. As if they couldn't leave.

I felt sorry for them, trapped and forgotten, and the more I looked at them, the more I was sure that once, long ago, other people had stood where we did. That they'd been the ones who'd built the Angel House. That they'd worshipped their own terrifying angels.

I told Ann what I thought after we both got burned across our thighs while practicing bomb-wearing, and she repeated what I said, leaving me to suffer through extra prayers to cleanse my heart and an empty plate during meals.

Mary told on me when she caught me in the kitchen trying to take a piece of bread on the fifth day of my cleansing, when I was so dizzy with exhaustion and hunger I could hardly stand.

"Why did you do that?" I said when she came into the study room as I was scrubbing the floor— it was decided I needed to cleanse myself and the house—and pointed at her skin, then mine. We weren't so different, she and I. We both had blood that wasn't from the People running through us. I thought that should mean something.

She was the only person I knew like me.

"Because of that," she said, echoing my pointing back. "Everything you do gets me judged, just as everything I do gets you judged. Someday you'll be glad I listened and obeyed when you wouldn't. When one of us has our beautiful, final day, and I hope I'm picked to go first, you'll see that our skin doesn't matter. You'll see that what we do matters. Who we are here matters."

I went back to scrubbing, but she didn't go away. She sat down and studied, moving her feet when I had to scrub the dirt out of the stones under them.

She was right about our skin meaning nothing, but not the way she wanted it to. All that time she spent studying to be an Angel, all the belief she had in what we were taught and in the Saints, and the People will remember me far longer than they ever will her. I'll be held up as a sign of what bad blood—blood from Keran Berj's world—does.

I'll be used as proof of how nothing in or from Keran Berj's world is worth keeping. There will be no more children like Mary or me, and not just because no one from Keran Berj's world has come up into the Hills for years. The People will never risk another Angel like me.

Mary lived for the People when they didn't want her, but in the end, what she did will be forgotten. It had already started to slip away—willed away, maybe—before I left.

I remember, though.

CHAPTER 12

 $\mathcal{J}$ erusha was Mary's calling.

Jerusha, Keran Berj's devoted disciple. A monster he'd created.

It was a surprise, her being sent to him. Her mother was like mine, one of those who'd come to the Hills thinking they could study how the People lived, a group devoted to peace when there was none to be found. But her mother didn't end up like mine. She lived, and was used hard by the Rorys.

The only reason Mary was even taken by the Angels is that she looked so much like someone from out of the Hills, from Keran Berj's world, that everyone agreed it was the proper thing, especially since she'd managed to live with no kin and survive.

And she believed. Inside Angel House, Mary heard all the stories and prayers she never had before, and grew to believe in the Saints and the People so much that she'd make her knees bloody kneeling and praying. It was the devotion—and how she looked, so pale, so much like them—that got her sent out first. That got her sent to Jerusha.

Ann thought Mary was planning on running away. Lily and I agreed Ann was just jealous that she wasn't called first. She thought it was her right, since she was the oldest, and she followed Mary around as soon as she was called, questioning her. She even dug through the bag Mary packed right in front of her, and, at the last prayer, chanted loudly about trust.

Mary ignored her until after the final words of that prayer, but when it was done and we were walking her outside, starting the final farewells, she grabbed Ann's arm and said, "I've got more cause to hate Keran Berj than you ever will. He said it was a good idea for my mother to come here, sent her and all her peace-loving friends into the Hills to—" She paused, and spat on the ground three times. "He's why I'm here. And that's why his beloved Jerusha will die."

"But freedom isn't about that," Ann said. "It's not about revenge. Your mother is nothing. Freedom is—"

"I know what freedom is," Mary said, and smiled like a Saint herself. "I go because I live for it. I live to serve the People as they see fit, and I will do what they and the Saints have called me to."

"Oh," Ann said, and looped Mary's arm through hers, leading the way to Mary's last meal before she was taken off the Hills. I stared after them until Lily came back and touched my arm.

"The bread will get cold if we have to wait for you," she said, and I nodded, still thinking about what I'd heard.

Wondering why Mary's freedom sounded so awful.

Why the thought of it made me want to scream.

Then she was gone, and it was ages—a winter so bitter it drove all of us, even the Angels, into the highest part of the Hills, and the start of a cold, wet spring—before we found out what happened to her.

CHAPTER 13

After the bomb, after I lived, after I saw Liam dead and took his belt, I went to Chris.

I'd waited till it was darkest night to go to him, scuttling around the City like a beetle and squinting at the signs Keran Berj had placed on everything. When I found him, he pulled me aside so fast I don't think anyone ever saw me, and he didn't speak until we were inside his house.

"So," he said, clapping me on the shoulder like the Rorys do when greeting someone after battle.

He knew our ways, it was true. But then he knew everyone's ways. And his voice was not warm with greeting.

He lit a match, and the glow of it was so bright after the dark I'd been stuck in for days that it hurt my eyes. I saw his mouth scowl down before the match burned out, and then I was shoved up against the wall, a knife nicking into my throat.

"What do you want?" he said, and I struggled around the fear that was turning my insides to liquid and dug out the cloth I'd been keeping tied tight to me.

I pushed it toward him. The knife pressed harder into my throat as he opened the cloth with his teeth. Even in the dark I could see the glint of the gold as it fell to the floor. We both looked at it lying there; the belt Liam had been dressed in, wrapped around his chill skin, and the tiny smoothed-out pebble of it Da had been given when he'd agreed that his line would end with him, that I was to be an Angel.

"I have to leave," I said, and he bent to pick up the gold, turning away from me in the dark, the knife gone from my throat as if it had never been there at all.

"And you want me to help you." He turned the pebble of gold over in his hand, the belt still on the floor, and I saw he knew what it was. What I was.

"Yes," I said, and he made a sound of disgust, thick in the dark, but kept the gold in one hand still, as if weighing it against me.

"Upstairs," he said after a minute. "Second door on the left. Leave your clothes in the hall to be burned."

In the morning, he brought me a dress, plum colored like a fresh bruise, and gave me a piece of bread. "I think I might have a use for you. You listen, you do what I say, and you leave when I tell you to go," he said. "Understand?"

And then I waited. And waited. I learned the City from a map he gave me to memorize until I could almost see the parks, the shopping district. The palace where Keran Berj lived.

I learned his house with its tiny, cramped rooms, most of which I only glimpsed. I dreamed of being sent away on a ship, wrapped up in a rug. They were one of the few things Keran Berj let go because others wanted them enough to pay prices I'd heard would feed everyone for years.

And then Chris finally told me something.

"You'll be leaving soon," he said one night, after letting me inside from the brief, dark stroll he let me have around the fenced-in square that was his yard. Fourteen steps from one end to the other. Ten across. "You'll go by train. Someone will be with you."

"But I—" I said, and broke off because I could

tell from his voice there was nothing I could say. No one like Chris would take in someone like me without conditions. No one was going to simply save me.

I had myself, though. I used to think that wasn't enough, but I knew better by then. I was all I had. All I'd ever had. And it would be enough. It had to be.

I would save myself.

CHAPTER 14

*I*n the train station, I waited with my papers.
Kerr's were tucked inside the daily paper. The only
one, the one with Keran Berj's picture beaming out
in grainy shades of black and white.

Chris had made me leave, finally and unexpect-
edly, pushing me out the back door when it was
barely light and I was still mostly asleep, pausing
only long enough to press papers and a few coins
into my hands as he said, "Keep your papers in

plain sight. You'll be searched, so don't hide the others on you. Buy a paper and put them in that. You're waiting for Kerr. He's your brother. When he comes, let him do the talking."

"How will I find him?" I said, only knowing that this Kerr was who Chris—and therefore I—had been waiting for. And that he hadn't come. I knew nothing else about him, not his real name, not even what he looked like.

"He'll find you," Chris said, and then shut the door in my face.

I was searched four times in the train station. The old woman who complained about how her joints ached, her back humped like pain had broken her, was searched six, although it was clear the soldiers only skimmed over her, afraid to touch too much. A man wearing a black hat, which I found was forbidden when one of the solders waved a long sheet of paper in the air and asked why the man hadn't read the latest Words from God that

Keran Berj had received, was searched eight times, and roughly, too.

Searching was like Liam hunting for me in bed, only better because I didn't end up with Liam puffing over me, closing his eyes to block out my face. I just had a soldier or two wondering out loud what I looked like under my skirts and a hand or two venturing up them. Though my heart hammered with worry over how Kerr hadn't come, and how I didn't know how to find him, the first time I was searched was the only time I was scared for myself.

I was scared because the soldiers kept poking and pinching me even though I stood there, patient like the People are, patient like I'd been taught was necessary. I didn't know why it seemed to drive them on, but then the old woman with the hump of pain on her back raised her hands to her face, shook like she was crying, and then looked at me.

I understood then, and so I pretended to cry,

pinching the skin of my right wrist as I twisted from side to side, from one set of arms to another, wailing like I would have done the day I met Liam if I'd thought my voice would have been heard at all.

The old lady was right. The soldiers grinned and backed away, pleased with my tears, and what fear I had vanished. I realized the soldiers truly weren't like the Guards. They were simply bored men standing around, and what they did was like what the younger Rorys, the ones in training, do when they ride through a village. They'll walk into houses and steal kisses or bread or both, and only for the fear it causes.

I didn't fear the soldiers like they wanted because my body had never been my own. It was the People's, always, and briefly belonged to Liam too. I never thought of it as something other than a vessel—an Angel is a messenger and nothing more—until I looked up at a cloudless blue sky and thought not of the Saints or even the People.

I just thought it was a pretty sky, and was glad to see it.

I realized I wanted to keep seeing it.

I had wanted things for myself before, but never like I wanted to keep seeing that sky. I didn't understand what it meant then.

What my choices would cost.

CHAPTER 15

Chris's house was strange. So many rooms, and all for one person. Two, if you counted me, but I knew neither of us did.

The City was strange too. It was orderly; so clean the streets appeared to shine, and all the buildings were a uniform gray, maybe colored by Keran Berj because he liked it, or maybe colored by the factories he'd built. Walking to the train station, I saw it all, and the City was dark and cold and so strangely sad—the slumped buildings that appeared to be homes but could have been anything, the golden statues of Keran Berj on almost every corner, and all the quiet, waiting people standing in orderly lines outside dark buildings.

Everything had its place, everyone had their place, and I could finally see why so many followed Keran Berj. He'd broken everyone, but more importantly, he'd broken the land. Everything around me was his creation.

Keran Berj's laws were stranger than I thought, though. The statues I knew about, of course, and the palace he lived in, the way he put his picture on everything. Bread. Wine bottles. Candy. But in the train station, as my papers were inspected and I listened to the soldiers argue over how to stamp them, trying to remember if Keran Berj wanted a circle or a square, I realized it was impossible to know all of Keran Berj's rules. There were too many, and they were always changing.

I wondered if that's what he wanted.

My scalp ached from the dye, which Chris had done the day before he'd sent me off in the dark, and I collected a circle, a square, and then a circle inside a square on my papers.

Kerr still did not come, but a man whose shoes made a sharp tick-tock noise as he walked did. He walked around the station twice, his shoes loud in the sudden, frightened silence, looking for something. The soldiers all stood stiff and unmoving while he did.

I wondered what Angel would be sent to meet the tick-tock man, and looked at the newspaper that held Kerr's papers. Next to the large, smiling picture of Keran Berj that I'd seen everywhere, on everything, there was a picture of a body—dressed in black and covered with medals—being lowered into the ground, Keran Berj standing beside it. Below the picture was a poem Keran Berj had written.

It was called "Memory." It was written in honor of the recently dead Minister of Defense. The word "freedom" was used in every line. I rubbed my right wrist and watched the man with the tick-tock shoes march to the station doors.

"Nari, Leji," he called, and two Guards came inside.

They walked over to the tick-tock man and listened as he spoke. Then they went down to the tracks and looked one way, then the other. They came back and as the frightened silence started to ease they made the old woman with the bent back stand up. One of the Guards hit her across the mouth, said, "Traitor." She swayed, and a child fell out of her coat, the lump on her back revealed as a small boy with bright blue eyes but hair and skin of the People.

The Rorys used to always spit when they saw me because my own eyes are blue.

The Guards did not spit. They simply took the boy and the woman outside. They did not come back.

There was no sign the child or woman had ever

been in the station. People moved into their seats as if they'd never existed.

I wanted to go, but I couldn't. My only option was to stay where I was and so I did. I sat, and I waited for the train to come.

Eventually, it did.

And so did Kerr.

CHAPTER 16

I heard the train first. There were no tracks where I lived, for even the man with the train, the one who had it before Keran Berj—even he recognized our land for what it was and let it be. Keran Berj had once tried to push rails into the first low swells of the Hills, but the land swallowed the spikes he tried to plant and the Rorys killed all his workers.

But I had seen trains. Though Keran Berj could

not reach the Hills, he reached up near them, and I'd glimpsed them off in the distance when I was little and still with Da. And then, when I was training to be an Angel, we all had to walk down from the Hills and see one passing by so that if we were asked about it, we could describe it, for it was one of Keran Berj's many sources of pride.

I had thought it a strange blot on the rolling brown grain of the plains below the Hills, and Ann and Lily and Mary and I had all talked about how noisy it was. But in the station it was so much louder than the far-off hum I'd heard. It sounded like the thunder from a hundred storms, and made the ground pulse, a strange, low throbbing that I couldn't hear, but could feel beneath my feet.

"Sister, I'm here," someone said as I stared. And then he hissed, "Where are my papers?" as arms pretended to hug me.

That was Kerr, finally arrived.

"Brother," I said, broken from the train's spell, and when I handed him the newspaper, his fingers slipped inside and pulled out the identification card and passes so fast I didn't even see it.

He elbowed me when I tried to look at his face and turned away, glanced at a couple waiting together and said, "Has someone told those two that Keran Berj frowns on public displays of affection?"

The soldiers, who had been watching us, blinked at him, at the loud sureness of his voice, and then turned toward the couple, who guiltily unclasped their hands and cringed.

"Don't stare at them," Kerr said to me. His voice was cold, ice cruel.

"I'm not yours to order," I said, and kept watching them.

He said nothing in reply and I thought for a moment that I'd surprised him, but when I glanced over at him he was looking at the newspaper, carefully folding it so that only the bright, glowing face of Keran Berj showed.

Now that I finally saw him, I realized he was

my age or a year or two older, and clearly carried not one drop of the People's blood. He was pale all over, hair and skin, and so far everything he'd done—the way he'd spoken to me, the way he'd eagerly and loudly, openly, turned on someone else—made me wonder why he would even need someone like Chris.

I wondered, but not enough to turn away. Not enough to try and fade into the crowd, to try and fade into the City, into some sort of shadow life.

I wanted more than that. I'd wanted it enough to find and endure Chris. To be here in the station. In the City.

So when the train opened its doors, I followed Kerr, and sat down beside him.

CHAPTER 17

*W*e were supposed to arrive at the border yester-
day, but everyone—especially the People—knows
that while Keran Berj may boast of the power of
his land, the might of his army, and the efficien-
cy of his train, he doesn't control all the land; his
army is nothing without his Guards and the certain death they bring, and the train runs more on
the whims of its tracks than on Keran Berj's will.

Well into the second day of a trip that was supposed to be done in one, the washroom has rapidly become something no one wants to brave unless they must. The men go with the soldiers to the back car and "water the ground," and the women take deep breaths and wade in to something fouler than even the worst animal pen.

All the other women seem less bothered by the filth and smell of the washroom than I am, as if a soldier leering is far worse than squatting over a hole so clogged with waste that it is seeping onto the floor. Perhaps all of them are used to obeying Keran Berj's ever-changing rules, to waiting in lines, to giving up everything he asks for his new statues or roads or whatever he wishes. Perhaps they truly only think of him.

I don't.

The train begins the slow grinding noises that means it is stopping, and out the window I see shadows of buildings, tiny against the dust-colored ground. We are deep into the desert now, land no one wants to live in, but it is home to those Keran

Berj wants isolated. Punished. Those who broke his laws are sent here, out into this hot, barren emptiness. Death comes for them but slowly, slowly.

I suspect Keran Berj likes that.

As the train lurches to a halt, people from the shimmer-haze of buildings stream out, red-faced from the sun as they shout through the windows.

"Water! Fresh, clean well water! Nothing added, and cold too!"

"Tea! Mint tea, soothing for the body and mind!"

"Dumplings! Fresh meat, fresh greens, boiled today!"

Windows on the train are pushed down, opened, and I watch the onion-smelling man bargain for a jar of water and a packet of dumplings, arguing furiously with a girl of no more than nine or ten, her pale skin peeling in strips down her face. I can see the angry red of her scalp through her bone-white hair, and touch my own in sympathy.

I do not buy anything. These people, these window flies, are here because they followed Keran

Berj blindly, and when he tossed them aside they were sent here. They were sent and they stay, living on their tiny, arid patches of land and doing nothing. They have no spirit.

Kerr buys things, though. Always, at every stop, even the first ones we made when the City was still in sight, shining statues of Keran Berj still watching over us. He bought overpriced fried puffs of dough and the little meat patties that people shape with spoons bearing Keran Berj's name, and fruit juices in cold, dripping cans printed with Keran Berj's face. He bought from fat, slow men and women, people who had plenty, who clearly knew ways to get around the ration system and would praise Keran Berj with one side of their mouth while the other counted out coins. I wondered how many of them reported to Chris in one way or another.

Now Kerr is buying water, mint tea, and two packets of dumplings, paying with coins that I still haven't figured out where he carries and thanking each person as if their desperation doesn't scream

from the gleam in their eyes to their shaking, skin-
ny hands and bodies.

No one gets on the train here.

No one gets off, either.

No one would ever willingly get off here.

Eventually, the soldiers get off the train and
push the people pressing against the windows
away. Kerr unwraps the dumplings before the
train starts rattling away, eating them in quick,
small bites. He eats more neatly than anyone I have
ever known, even Mary, who could act so fine you
would think she'd gone to the special school Keran
Berj built for girls he thought would serve well as
tour guides for the few outsiders let in.

He offers me two, and I eat them because it is
stupid to refuse food, even if the rice is not spiced
properly and the meat tastes of cow and not the
goat that it should be.

I miss the strangest things. Rice with red pep-
per cut so fine it looks like flakes. The strips of
goat in the stew we ate to mark the arrival of win-

ter. The smell of the Hills when spring was coming and the earth was damp with promise, like a girl is supposed to be on her first night with her pledged.

The way Da would sometimes talk of my mother when I was young and drink set him that way. How his eyes would go all soft and far away. His obsession for her—his willingness to claim her for himself when he didn't need to and to talk of her after she'd gone—destroyed him in the eyes of his family. They never acknowledged him again, not even after I became an Angel.

They never once even looked at me.

I wanted to understand what he felt for her, but I didn't. He claimed her and she'd chosen to leave him and this world, slipped away to have me, mouth gritted around a rag so Da wouldn't hear her scream and come find her.

After I came and she was gone, bled out bone white, I was his penance. I was the price he paid for what he felt for her, and he did right by putting me to good use. By taking me to the Angel House.

By making sure death was all that waited for me too.

CHAPTER 18

*K*err eats the other packet of dumplings after the train has been laboring acros the desert, after the soldiers have passed through again, not even looking at our papers. They smell of fresh meat, and some of them have crumbs on their shirts.

Food must have been loaded on for them at the last stop. I've heard stories about what they eat. Bread made with flour so fine it makes loaves that don't go hard the moment they cool. Fried meat patties as large as my palm, and fresh greens even in the winter.

"Why do you think those people sell their own food?" Kerr asks, and I shrug, take the two dumplings he is holding out to me.

"To wait in the sun like that, for so few coins . . ." He shakes his head. "If the old man I bought these dumplings from sells fifty a day—and how could he, when only one train passes through and everyone else is selling too—he would make less than what everyone who lives in the City is paid for putting up posters of Keran Berj in their homes."

I shrug again. Talk about the window flies is stupid. They paid for following Keran Berj, and if they want to use what food they are rationed to make money, it is their concern, not mine. They are still stuck in his world, thinking of coins and how to get things. They sell their food without understanding where it comes from, without seeing that land must be cherished.

"They don't get ration cards out here, you

know," he says, as if he knows what I've thought, plucking the dumpling wrapper out of my hand and smoothing it flat across his knee. "They don't get anything. They're forced to live out here, in this heat, in this land where almost nothing grows. They struggle to just live."

"They chose their path," I say.

He looks at me. I cannot read his face, see only a flicker of something in his eyes, and add, "And as Keran Berj wishes, he is to be obeyed," for good measure. I know the lines of praise as well as anyone on this train. I just don't believe them.

I never have, and am sure Kerr once did. I look at him again, so well-fed sleek even now.

"You feel for them?" I say, knowing my voice is mocking and thinking of the couple in the train station, of how he turned on them. How I am sure he has certainly sent people out here, or worse.

"You don't understand anything," he says, his voice quiet, and looks out the window. I do too, wondering what it would be like to live with nothing but sand and heat, to not have trees and soil that thrives. It would be hard to love this land.

Hard to live in it. And with no ration cards, no soil to grow things in . . .

The next time we stop, I use one of the few coins Chris gave me to buy a piece of bread from a woman who would be about my mother's age, if she had lived. The woman's face is narrow, bone-gaunt, and when she passes me the bread, I see the tendons in her arms, as if there is nothing else lying between her skin and bones.

"Take it back," I tell her, and her eyes widen. She shakes her head, says, "It is good, I promise you. It is good bread."

"No," I say, pressing it into her hand. "I mean you should eat it."

"You gave me your coin," she says, and when I nod, she frowns, confused, and then disappears into the crowd as if I might come after her and take the coin back. As if I might grab the bread she was willing to give me, the bread I see her cramming into her mouth as if she can't be bothered to taste it.

As if she is starving.

"Now you understand," Kerr says when the train starts moving again. His voice holds no smugness, though, and when I look over at him, he is fiddling with the collar on his shirt, opening and closing the top button over and over again.

CHAPTER 19

*W*hen the sun finally starts to set, it's oddly bright on the train, as if the last moments of daylight are somehow captured by the metal and then pushed through the windows in bright shards.

Kerr is staring out the window still, as if he can see past the light, as if he can see something off in the distance.

I don't know how he does it. My eyes water like

I'm weeping, and yet he, so soft-looking, so pale and round-cheeked, is fine.

"You must be used to very strong light," I say, wiping my eyes.

"Yes," he says, and his voice is full of pain.

The door at the far end of the car opens, and the blond soldier from before comes back. He leans over us, smelling of fresh air, food, and drink—so much better than I smell now, after hours of sweat and the muck on my skirt.

"Would you like something to eat?" he says.

"Food?" Kerr says, and I look at him, at the rounded curves of his face, gentle chin and cheeks that do not stretch tight over the bones. Soft, so soft. I despise how weak he is. I cannot wait to leave him behind.

"Food," the soldier says, low-voiced, and Kerr glances out the window one more time and then stands up, smiling. His smile is a polished, gleaming thing, practiced and beautiful, and I try not to stare as he says, "I'll bring you something back, sister."

His smile is brilliant. His voice is warm.

His eyes are cold. Dead.

I wait until he's gone, and then make the sign to ward off evil three times. I have to do it with my hand held under my skirt so no one else will see, and I don't know if it will work or not. I don't know if protection works when the Saints have turned their faces away from you.

But then, I made the sign plenty of times before and it never protected me from anything.

Kerr comes back when I am half asleep, my eyes still stinging from the setting sun, and I squint at him.

He sits down, looking away. Looking out the window once more. It is growing dark now. There is nothing to see, but still he looks.

I rub my eyes and look at him again. Kerr's mouth and chin are red, a strange sick color, like

the inside of a cut, and he smells like Liam did after he came to bed and spoke of Sian.

Kerr sees me looking at him and turns to
face me.

I am the first to drop my eyes.

The soldier who'd stopped to talk to us comes
through the car a little later with a few others,
whistling at something that's said as he tosses a
piece of bread at Kerr.

"You're handing out food now?" one of the other soldiers says, and the one who tossed the bread
laughs and says, "Payment. Besides, it fell on the
floor near the passenger washroom. You want it?"

The soldiers laugh and go on their way. Kerr
tears the bread in half, wiping it clean, and puts a
piece of it in his mouth.

Then he offers the other half to me. No words,
just puts it in one hand and holds it out.

I look at him. The color on his face has faded.
There are bits of grit on his pant legs, ground in
around the knees.

I take the bread and eat it.

Kerr's eyes widen, but he doesn't say anything. After a while, he looks at the floor, tracing the button at the top of his shirt, the one that presses into his throat.

I watch him for a while and then the heat and the sensation of food in my stomach closes my eyes again.

"You do what you must in order to survive," he says when I wake up, gasping, from a dream of blood-dark flowers wrapping around me. The train is still rattling hotly over the tracks, pushing through the dark desert.

"Yes," I say, looking at the bright stars and thinking of learning how to die. Of stiff white fabric billowing around as wires rubbed against my leg.

Of where I am now.

"I'd kill you to save myself, you know," he says, so quietly his voice sounds like part of the train's low, constant throb.

I yawn. I am here, trapped in an escape, and I'm beyond fearing words now. I have never heard many kind ones anyway.

He grabs my arm, as if that will somehow make me feel his threat. I push it off and grab his hand in return, bending the pale, soft fingers back a little. I can't do more than that. Not now. We still have the border to reach. To cross.

I can't see his face, but his fingers, captured in my hand, are shaking.

I wonder what it's like to have violence be new and terrifying as I fall back asleep.

Even in my dreams, I can't picture it.

CHAPTER 20

*E*arly morning, my eyes gritty from dark dreams, and the train has stopped again.

I tense, wondering if something has happened. If the Guards have somehow found out about me. Come for me.

But there are no Guards to see, only the train crew. They are standing around the tracks, pointing at something and then arguing with each other.

My legs hurt from trying to keep my feet off

the floor. I give in, relax. The pain is almost worth it. I cross one foot over the other, pressing down layers of skirt that have popped up around me like small hills.

The skirt I'm wearing was yellow-green, like leaves as they are about to turn. Chris gave it to me when he woke me up and pushed me out the door, but it's turned darker now, damp with sweat and grime. The bottom, which has brushed against the washroom floor, is something I will never touch again. I will peel the skirt away from me once I am over the border and find something clean to wear. Something that isn't from Keran Berj's world.

Or mine.

I want something new.

I look at the bottom of the shoe that isn't resting on the train floor. It's started to melt. I check the other one and it is melting too, the image of the sun that has been stamped onto the bottom swirling into a collapsed circle.

Beside me, Kerr sleeps, mouth open and closed eyes still turned toward the window.

After a while the soldiers get off the train and squint into the distance, looking one way, then another, until they all set off to the right. The deeper into the desert we go, the faster this takes—everything is easier to see because there is nothing but sun and sand, nowhere to hide—and within minutes they are all in line for the water pump. They stand, waiting, with flasks that they will fill before returning to the train. A few talk in a knotted cluster as they wait, nodding and smoking their thin pipes stamped with Keran Berj's smiling face.

Everyone on the train watches them. All of us stare out the windows, thinking of all that water. Sometimes a soldier will fill his flask too full, and drops will spill onto the ground.

There is such stillness then, such silence, as we all long to catch those drops. To feel cold water on our skin. In our mouths.

The pumps do not have Keran Berj's face or his smile or his sun on them. They are solid-looking, worn with age, from a time before all of this, and I think of what the man who made them would do to Keran Berj.

That man could find water in the desert and built this winding metal path across the land. He would crush Keran Berj like a bug, grind him between his fingers until there was nothing left but dust.

I smile, and Kerr wakes with a start, gasping. When he sees my face, whatever he was dreaming of falls away and he follows my eyes, sees what I'm looking at and then elbows me once, hard. I ignore him, but when he does it again I follow his eyes, which are not looking out the window, but at the door.

The soldiers are coming back, invigorated with fresh air and water, and I put my papers on my right knee and wait while they scratch themselves and then decide to look at our papers yet again.

They spend a lot of time talking to some people at the front of the car, two women traveling with a small, gloriously dressed child who must be important because he is given water from the soldiers' flasks.

I want the train to start moving again and shift in my seat. As I do, I feel sweat drip down the back of my neck. I think of the dye yet again and lift one hand, tuck the short length of one side of my hair behind my ear, and check my fingers.

I think they are lighter than they were before. My stomach knots.

I have light hair, but I am not sure if it is still light enough, not light like it should be if I want to walk across the border and have the Guards believe I will come back.

And now the soldiers are coming this way; I see their feet, I see them, and they will see me, my hair, and—

"Sister," Kerr says, tapping my head playfully before his hand rests on my knee, digging into the bone, a warning. "Someone is speaking to you."

I look up and see a soldier, bitter-eyed with a sneer of a mouth, staring at me, eyes roaming across me.

I smile at him. Smiles are easy. I smiled when Da's family would walk by me and pretend I wasn't there, even when it was known that I'd been called. I smiled after Da handed me over at Angel House and the one who led me inside said, "I can't believe we're taking another one with bad blood. Saints bless me, but I don't want to spend forever by your side." I smiled when I'd walk through camp and people would greet me but never ask me to visit, would turn their faces away, duty done. I smiled when Liam dug his fingertips into my sides to hold me beneath him.

I smiled when I wrapped a bomb around my leg and was told to go, that I was lucky because it was truly a glorious day to die.

"You look thirsty," the soldier says. "Are you?"

I nod, because I have heard his unpleasantness, his mockery, his disdain taunting voice a thousand times over, in Mary saying "You don't try hard enough" when I would frown and she would stare, blank-faced, at the Rorys spitting three times whenever she and I walked by. In Liam saying "I'm so tired of pretending you're Sian. I pray every day that the Saints will take you soon." In Ann and Lily noticing how pale I'd gotten before I left, how they smiled and said, "Shut away for a few days, and now you look just like one of them."

"I could give you some water, if you want." The words are kind. His voice isn't.

I look at my hand. There is nothing on it. My hair is fine. I don't look like I'm from the Hills. I look like one of Keran Berj's kind, his obedient sheep slaves.

I look like I am used to hearing orders and obeying them.

The thing is, I am.

CHAPTER 21

I was told what to do—what I was—so many times. I had been told what would happen to me so many times. I was raised knowing the Angels were reminders that the People would never give way. I was raised knowing my life was to be used in hopes of changing the world.

I was to keep nothing in my heart but devotion. No love, no hate, no room for anything else but what I was to do. How I was to serve.

So when the soldier gestures for me to follow him, I do.

I have no other choice.

I only had one once, and it has brought me here, to me following behind this soldier, resignation heavy in my heart.

But the soldier surprises me.

I expect to be dragged into their washroom—which I am—but instead of reaching under my skirt he asks about my imaginary sister, the one who has a baby due very soon.

"Was she sick when she was first carrying the child?" he says. "Did it—did it make her ill?"

I nod slowly, staring at him warily and trying to hide my surprise at his question. Every woman I have ever seen with a rounded belly in the Hills spoke of being ill. Some with pride, some with res-ignation. But they all spoke of it. They all knew it would happen.

He blows out a breath. "Was there . . . what did you do about it? What is there to do to fix it?"

I cannot picture this soldier with a family, a pregnant wife, sister, niece—anything. He is Keran Berj's creature and no more, except here he is, talking to me.

Asking for my help.

I clear my throat.

"Rest," I say. "Bland foods. Sickness is normal. It passes."

He stares at me for so long I think I have said the wrong thing but after a moment he hands me his flask. He pulls it away after I take three swallows. The water is so cold it bites into my teeth. It is glorious. I want more.

"You weren't that helpful," he says when I look at the flask, and then opens the door, pushes me out. His hand is heavy on my shoulder as he walks me back to my seat, and as I sit, he presses something into my hand.

I wait until after he is gone to open my fingers.

Sitting on my palm is a waxed packet of rice

balls. The rice is fresh, the grains still puffed and not shriveled from the heat.

"Don't cry," Kerr whispers, and the pinch he delivers to my arm is almost enough to mask the note of fear in his voice.

"I'm not," I whisper back, but there is something wet on my face, and I am.

"Are you . . . hurt?" Kerr says, low-voiced.

I shake my head. How can I say that three sips of water and these rice balls—gained from answering a simple question—are the most kindness I have ever gotten from anyone? How can I say that someone asking me for advice is the most I have ever been judged worthy of?

"If you aren't hurt, then why are you—?" Kerr says, a whisper against my ear, and I turn, look at him.

He draws back as if I have hit him, and I know what he sees. I can't hide my surprise now. Or my pain.

I shove a rice ball in my mouth. I offer him the other one and wonder if his softness will make him reach for it, or if he will turn away.

He opens the top button on his shirt instead, and as he does, I see raw red skin.

I see why Chris told me he had a use for me.

I am traveling with Jerusha.

I am traveling with death itself.

JERUSHA

CHAPTER 22

*O*nce, back when I was still living with Da, some of Keran Berj's followers thought he had too much power. They looked at his gold statues and palace and realized he cared only for himself, not them. They never made any overtures to us, but we heard of them. We knew they wrote letters and smuggled them out. We heard that faraway countries asked to send inspection teams to visit, to see if life under Keran Berj's thumb was as sweet as he claimed.

Keran Berj replied by saying he didn't believe in violence, and that he and his people, his land, would not participate in any ongoing wars or in any wars that were to be. Then he sent money for "relief" or "care" or "rebuilding" to every nation that had ever questioned him. He said there were tragedies going on around the world and "we" only wanted to help. He even built a glass tower and had the word PEACE carved into it to show how much he loved everyone.

No inspection teams came, and Keran Berj sent his Guards out to round up everyone who had spoken out against him. They say the piles of bodies in the City were so thick that entire streets were closed. In the end, rather than bury the dead, Keran Berj simply lit part of the City on fire, and built a park covered with statues of him over its remains.

And then he passed laws. It was illegal to speak against Keran Berj or even mention him to outsiders. It was illegal to even think ill of him, and those he thought might have died in mass hangings that everyone in the City was required to attend.

He also sent Special Instruction Units to visit every school, and each child was given a copy of stories he'd written about how Keran Berj was now both mother and father to all because his God had told him so. There was more—we had one of the booklets, and all the Angels had to read it to understand what we were facing—but the very last thing Keran Berj said was that everyone had a role to play in keeping the world safe, and that if you ever saw or heard someone say something bad about him, you should write him a letter. He said he would read each and every one because he knew he could trust his children.

Lots of letters were written, and people— mostly older sisters and brothers, but some parents and a few aunts and uncles and grandparents— were taken in for questioning. Nothing serious was found—a few people were fined, or were reassigned to different, lesser jobs—but each child who turned in a family member got a package of sticky honey sweets and a little cap with Keran Berj's face on it, and so more letters were written.

The sticky sweets and hats made children happy and families scared, but Keran Berj wasn't happy. He was sure there were still plots against him, but he could find nothing. He tried hanging his son for thinking badly of him, but it didn't help him find anything. It just scared people.

After that, he started giving long speeches about the losses he'd suffered for God and everyone who lived in his land. He even said he was praying for the People. Of course, he also called us "savage killers" and promised to bring "swift and sure" justice if we didn't listen and obey him, but still. He spoke of us and there was talk among the People that perhaps he could be moved against. That all his killings had finally frightened his people enough to act. To rise up.

Then Jerusha Nichola wrote a letter to Keran Berj.

Jerusha Nichola lived in the City. He had met Keran Berj twice, and had even taken a tour of his office with a few other select children. His father, Pazi, was Chief Inspector for Factories, and his mother, Eliana, was Director of Music. Pazi made sure the factories ran the way Keran Berj wanted. He was also responsible for sending those who knew how to make the goods the factories churned out to a hot death in the desert. He made it so Keran Berj was the only choice for everything in life.

Eliana wrote songs for Keran Berj. None of them are sung now, but Keran Berj's "Song of Praise" was her creation, its refrain a simple chant about Keran Berj's glory that all were once required to learn. With consequences if one didn't.

Pazi and Eliana did not like Keran Berj. They had both written letters to outside governments, and paid a fortune in bribes to make sure their names were never mentioned to him.

They thought they were safe because they'd paid so much money, and because Keran Berj killed others and not them, but after Keran Berj killed his own son they worried that perhaps someone would talk about what they'd done. They decided to offer to go on a diplomatic trip to a country eager for trade with Keran Berj, and never come back.

They kept all this secret. Not even the servants they had working for them, raw-boned country girls whom Pazi molested in the pantry and Eliana beat for not being quick enough with dinners, knew.

But their son knew. He heard them talking when he was supposed to be asleep. And so he wrote Keran Berj a letter.

His parents were arrested the day they were supposed to leave.

CHAPTER 23

*T*here's a famous picture of Jerusha's parents after their arrest, their faces crumpled with fright as Keran Berj watches with one arm around little Jerusha, who smiles proudly at the camera and doesn't look at his parents at all.

Keran Berj made that photo famous because he had it turned into posters that were placed everywhere. He even had soldiers nail them into the lowest lying trees in the Hills—after first killing them by pouring chemicals into the ground so their very roots would sicken and die.

We killed all the soldiers who we caught doing that—they were not Guards, and were no match for the Rorys—and used the posters to write our own messages. I even got to do one because we had so many, and I remember carefully writing RORYS FIGHT FOR FREEDOM! in hopes of a bit of praise from Da or even one of the women watching us because I was there, trying to be what I was supposed to be. Because every child was helping out, every child was showing that the People stick together.

There was no praise, but I liked being with everyone else, being a part of the People without question for once. I still remember how we all looked at the other side of the poster—at Jerusha smiling while his parents were being taken from him, and how all of us, even the older boys, the ones who went on to die in battle as Rorys when

I was learning how to die myself—and made the sign to ward off evil.

Jerusha's Law was passed the day before Jerusha's parents were hanged, and Jerusha was there when Keran Berj raised his hand and ordered the ropes dropped around their necks. He was there when their necks snapped. He was there, standing next to Keran Berj, when they died, mouth full of honey candy and a smile on his face.

Keran Berj made a speech afterward and talked about how brave Jerusha was. He showed off Jerusha's neck, which was red, an open sore rubbed raw by rope. Jerusha's parents had escaped the night before they were hanged and tried to kill their own son the way they knew they would die. Keran Berj said Jerusha was lucky to have lived, and Jerusha smiled.

Jerusha was a vision of the future, Keran Berj said, and then Jerusha himself called his parents' death a blessing. We burned all the papers we found proclaiming that, for while Keran Berj was evil, Jerusha was beyond that. To be so young and so cruel—he was the end of the world made flesh.

We were not the only ones horrified by Jerusha. The letters written by children slowed to a trickle when his parents were arrested, and stopped after their execution. Keran Berj and his God could claim such things were necessary, but it was easy to see that if every child became Jerusha, all would eventually die. And Keran Berj would let it happen.

We saw that and all thought as soon as it sank in that we, the People, were the only ones strong enough to say that Keran Berj was wrong in voices other than whispers, that others would join us.

No one did, and the only smart thing I ever heard Da say was during this time. All of the People had gathered to discuss sending Rorys to villages to try and recruit spies, and after it had been discussed for one day, then two, Da stood up, crabby from being without drink, and spat out, "Following us is certain death. We go to that willingly, but his people won't. They're too scared. That's what the little monster did for Keran Berj, scared them so hard they'll follow him no matter what. It's hard to believe you can be free when you know Keran Berj has made it so you aren't safe with your own family."

Everyone shouted Da down, but when a group went out, they were greeted with stones and whatever weapons the village they went to could find. As if Keran Berj's loving care, with his endless demands for money and worship, and his creation of a world where a boy would happily help kill his own parents, was something worth protecting.

Da took me off to be an Angel soon after that, and Jerusha seemed to disappear. Once in a while he'd show up on posters the Rorys would bring back from fighting, and they were put in Angel House for us to study. The picture was always the same, the little boy with the honeyed smile as his parents died, but we all learned Jerusha went to the Keran Berj Academy and spent his summers as a Keran Berj Junior Volunteer Soldier. He was an example to be watched and every year, on the anniversary of his parents' death, he and the Minister of Defense would visit Keran Berj and sing the new True Song of Praise.

Some of Keran Berj's followers whispered that Jerusha was dead, but we knew better. Keran Berj only showed pictures of himself when he was young and first came to power. He tried to freeze himself as he was, to act as if he would never age, and he needed Jerusha to be forever young too, because the moment he stood for—the deaths he willingly caused—still struck people cold.

And with Jerusha kept forever young in everyone's eyes, Keran Berj could use him again. Older and unseen, Jerusha could again do what he had all those years ago. He could be sent out to destroy. He could even come to us, claiming to be a simple soldier wanting a new, true life. And as he reached an age where that was possible, the Rorys killed any young men who came to us claiming they wanted to escape Keran Berj's world.

It wasn't enough, and so then an Angel was chosen to find him, to stop him.

Mary was sent.

And she failed.

CHAPTER 24

I make the signs to ward off evil at Jerusha, not caring if anyone sees, and he grabs my hand. His hand is soft, the skin smooth like a child's. Pampered from killing for Keran Berj, from being in his care. It makes my stomach roll, a lazy flip that sends the rice I just ate rolling up into my throat.

"I'm not—I'm—" he says, and I pull my hand away.

"You are." I cannot touch Jerusha. Even I am not that soured in the eyes of the Saints.

And yet I am with him. I am with Jerusha. Jerusha, who killed his parents. Jerusha, who lives in one of Keran Berj's many palaces, who lives closer to Keran Berj than someone like the Minister of Culture could ever dream.

If I get up now and run, I may be able to throw myself off the train before anyone can stop me. Death would be quick. Maybe.

And even if it wasn't, even if I somehow landed safely and ended up slowly dying in the desert, it would be better than whatever Jerusha has planned for me.

"Stay still before you get us both killed," Jerusha hisses, and he is holding my hand again, his grip surprisingly strong. His voice is so cold.

He is Death, and he is here. He has come for me.

I stay still.

I wait for what I've always been told is my fate.

CHAPTER 25

The train lets out a low, piercing scream as it rounds a corner, and there is still nothing to see but sand. The wind blows it like dust up against the windows.

I look at Jerusha.

I have seen death many times but when it came for me, I did not want it. I turned away. I ran.

And now it has caught up to me again, sits wearing the face of a pale, hollow-eyed boy with a red scar around his neck from where his own parents tried to stop him and failed. With a raw wound on top of it, a gift from an Angel.

From Mary.

I touch my own throat and Jerusha smiles at me. It is a cold smile.

I look away, shaking.

"We can't all be loved," he says. "Some of us are just . . . wrong. Keran Berj used to tell me that somewhere two souls were crying because they had a little boy who said he loved them."

"He lied," I say, trying to keep my voice strong. To be strong even now. "Why would they cry for you?"

"Why would they?" he mutters, and then looks at me. "They wouldn't, of course. They don't."

"I won't tell you where the People are."

He shrugs. "I don't care about that."

"You'll never find them. They don't leave paths, don't need trails. They're like ghosts, they're—"

"Silent warriors, the Rorys protected by the

Saints, I know," he says. "The People, beloved by the Hills and all that. If you care for them so much, why did you leave? What did you do? Draw maps in the dirt for Guards in order to get enough food to make your stomach stop shrieking in protest for a day or two?"

I stare at him.

"It happens at times, and besides, we all know you're starving," he says. "How can you not, living around all those trees? No proper ground to plant, no spaces to stay in and work the soil, make it your own."

"The earth belongs to itself, and I would never—I'm not like you."

"But you're here, aren't you?" he says, and leans forward, looks into my eyes. I draw back, but not before I see they are brown, like I wish my own were.

"I wouldn't—if I'd known you were—"

"What? If you'd known I was to travel with you, you'd have stayed behind?"

"Yes."

He blinks. "You could have . . . . you could have gone home?"

I swallow. "The People . . . we don't take life or those of others lightly, for we are not to judge anyone's path or worth. We are not like you."

He grins, laughter stretching his mouth wide, though he holds the sound inside, muting it to a silent push of air. His breath smells like mint.

"No?" he says, and I think of the Rorys discussing their fights, their kills. Of how the People would sing the numbers of the dead. Of how I learned the best ways to kill my target and as many of those around him as I could.

"We believe in what we fight for," I say. "We fight for freedom, to live as we will. All else must be set aside for that."

"Freedom depends on setting aside everything in its name," he says.

"That's what I said."

"No," he says. "That's what Keran Berj said

right after he said God told him he was to rule for a thousand years."

"That's not the same thing." It can't be. I don't want it to be.

"Yes," he says. "It is. It's exactly the same. You kill, we kill, we all mourn the dead and then send more off to die."

"Not you."

"No," he says. "Of course I don't. You've heard all about me, after all. Everyone has. But you—do you feel bad for those who have been killed?"

"I—" I say, and then stop. I know what he is doing. I know how Keran Berj works, how he tries to twist things around. He has everyone except the People following him. And here, next to me, is the one who killed his own family for him. His voice is not the truth, and Jerusha does not know I was an Angel.

"You were supposed to die, weren't you?" he says, touching his collar again. "And now that you haven't, you're not worthy to go back to the Hills.

Not worthy of living in the dirt. How do they do it? How do they get you Angels to talk like that? To believe that?"

"I'm not . . ." I say, and trail off when he looks at me because I see that he knows. He knows everything about me. What I was.

What I didn't do.

CHAPTER 26

*H*ow do you know about . . . about me?" I say, and there is no strength in my voice anymore.

"Why else would you be here?" he says. "If death was what you wanted, you wouldn't have gone to Christaphor. You wouldn't be on this train. You failed at your calling?"

"I—No. Yes."

"Both?"

I force myself to stay still. To not flinch. I can

see why Keran Berj loves him so, this cold boy. "I know all about your world. I know all about you."

"Of course you do," he says quietly, and touches his collar once more, fingers pressing against the button that holds it closed, against the wound that lies underneath. "You were trained for it. I know that."

"I've seen what you've created," I tell him. "I've been to one of your villages. I've seen a silent crowd watch as someone with power came, a Minister of Culture. I saw them say nothing about how round he was, fat from food that had to be given to Keran Berj no matter what because it's why he says his God wants him to have. I saw a crowd that looked and said nothing."

"They would die if they said anything."

"And that's your doing, isn't it?"

He looks at me, his face very still.

"In part," he says after a moment. "It is. You failed. Did you know that? The Minister lives."

I stare back at him.

"Yes," I say. "I know. The bomb failed."

I am dead. But then, I have been dead from the moment he came to me in the train station, haven't I? I take a deep breath.

"I—I watched the Minister. I watched him rise to speak. When he did I looked up at the sky and it was so blue, like another world, a better one, was there behind it, and I thought, I'll be there soon, I'll be there forever and everyone I know will be there forever too, and then I—" I stop.

"Then what?"

I shake my head. I'm done talking. I've said too much, more than I have ever said to anyone, but when I look at him, I see that he wants to know more. He wants to hear my story. I don't know why.

I just know no one else ever has.

"I didn't want it," I whisper. "Not death, not forever with the Saints. I didn't want any of it. I never . . . it was what I had to do but not—"

"What you wanted."

I stare at him.

"No," I finally say. "It wasn't. But now I'm— now I'm here. If I'd just gone back, if I could—"

"They'd kill you," he says. "And you know it because you're here. Your People won't rule with any kindness if they ever destroy Keran Berj, at least not for others. They'll save it all for the land."

"And you think everyone is treated kindly now? Have you seen what Keran Berj does to those he claims to love?"

"Yes," he says slowly, and turns away, looks out the window. "I have."

I take a deep breath. It is time, and it was foolish of me to think I could ever escape this moment.

"Will you—if you could just have the Guards come and get me now, get it over with. If you could—if you could have it end quickly," I say, trying to keep my voice from shaking. Trying to not sound like I am begging.

But I am.

He turns and looks at me, surprise on his face.

"Do you—you really think anyone is after you? You maimed the Minister of Culture and nothing more. You think the Minister of Culture truly matters to Keran Berj? You think he can't be replaced by any number of people?"

"But you're . . . "

"I know who I am."

"And the Guards. They have special orders about the People. I've seen them come to the Hills. They've tried to kill us all."

"Oh, they'd kill you if they found you," Jerusha says. "But Keran Berj doesn't want your blood. He wants the person who killed the Minister of Defense. He wants the person who took the codes the Minister carried, the ones that open all the doors to all of Keran Berj's secret lairs."

He smiles, and it is a horrible thing, crooked and furiously, savagely angry.

"He wants me."

CHAPTER 27

The train slows down once more and Jerusha sits up straighter, fingering his collar again.

We've reached another village but this one is smaller than the last, smaller than any of the others I've seen. Smaller and more desperate, hands pressed against the train windows before we've even stopped.

I watch Jerusha, but he does nothing, gestures for no one. He doesn't even buy anything, just keeps touching his collar, and so I take out the last of the coins Chris gave me.

I lean toward the window, toward the out-stretched hands pressed against it, and Jerusha puts his hand on my arm.

"We aren't supposed to stop here," he whispers.

I look at him and realize he is afraid. Under the softness that hides a heart that would let him watch his parents die, under the iciness and fright-eningly, sharply acute tongue—under all of that is something human.

He fears for himself, for he is trying to escape as well, and for now I am safe with him because of that.

I must also show him that he cannot rule me. I am done being what others will.

I lower the window and argue with a tall, bone-thin man over the price of a bottle of mint tea. The bottle is old, ringed with marks of past teas around the bottom, and the man has the same dark-red-earth skin of the People.

He is asking for too much money, for a thief's amount really, but I nod and start to hand over my coins. He looks at me, then reaches out and tugs my hair, grinning as I start to move away.

Only the People know that a woman should not show her hair in public, much less let a stranger touch it. A girl from Keran Berj's world would let her hair show and so I make myself smile at him.

He smiles back.

"Two coins, Hill girl," he says, lowering his price by more than half, and I stare at him, frozen, for this man knows who I am, that I am not from the City or any part of Keran Berj's world.

"It's safe," he says, pointing at the bottle, but I know he means something else. "I drink this tea all the time. Very refreshing for a long trip. Cold."

I hand over the coins.

"Blessings," he says, and presses the bottle into my hands. "May the Saints guide you well on your journey."

"And you on yours," I say, the proper response,

and Jerusha pulls me back inside so fast my head bumps against the window. My vision spots yellow-red, pain, and when I can see again the man is gone, vanished into the crowd, and Jerusha is holding the tea.

"You know him?" Jerusha says, and I shake my head, reaching for the bottle.

"No, but he knew I am—was—"

"Stop," Jerusha says, and eyes the people getting on, shoving the tea onto the floor, under the empty seat in front of me.

When I reach for it, he puts a hand on my arm, whispers, "Don't."

There is so much urgency in his voice that I still. Stop.

There are two people getting on the train, one an older man with a pinched face, an official clearly on a tour of places no one wants to see, most likely as a punishment. The other passenger is a woman who is finely dressed, no desert dust clinging to her clothes at all. Her hair is a little longer and a little lighter than Chris made mine, and I think about the dye once again. About how I am not who the papers I carry say I am. About what will happen when Jerusha speaks of me.

"Get up," Jerusha says, low-voiced, and then shoves me when I don't, yanking me up. My eyes burn but I will not cry. I will not.

A soldier comes up from the end of the car and says, "What are you doing?"

I freeze.

CHAPTER 28

I am frozen, terrified, but Jerusha's face shifts before my eyes, becomes weary.

"My sister, she snores," he says with a sigh, pointing at me. "And after two days—well, I must sleep before we reach the border and deal with bringing my other sister back to Keran Berj."

He nudges me aside and says to the soldier, "I brought her to help out, but she just sleeps and now I can't, and she simply doesn't understand that I must rest. I know I will be forced to argue with those—" He gestures off into the distance, toward where the train is slowly moving. "And so I must be ready for them."

The soldier nods, takes my elbow and pulls me into the aisle. "I have a sister myself, and as for what you're facing—well, Keran Berj is right that we should not trust others, isn't he? They just try to take away everything, like those People with their . . . ways." He spits three times, and it mists over my face, lands on my melting shoes.

"Truth, indeed," Jerusha says. "My poor sister is trapped, wanting to come home, but is she believed? No." He lowers his voice. "We even have a letter from Keran Berj himself about her, for her husband is . . . well. You understand, surely." He pulls a piece of paper with a heavy wax seal out of his pocket.

The soldier's mouth drops open. "I've never seen one of those before."

"Me either," Jerusha says. "I've been afraid to touch it, for it was in Keran Berj's hands, and his hands—"

"Touch God," the soldier says, wonder in his voice. "Well, you must sleep, then." He turns to me, points toward the back of the train car. "Go to the last seat and sit down."

I do. I sit and now I'm close enough to the door that if a soldier comes I could slip through, following him, and perhaps make it to the end of the train. I will say I need the washroom. Something. Anything.

But once I am off the train, if I live past the fall onto the tracks—where will I go? Keran Berj teaches many lessons to his followers, but the main one—and one Jerusha helped him teach—is that no one is safe. The man I saw back in the last village wished me luck, but he would not want me in his house, not even for a night. It would be noticed, a stranger coming in. It would mean death for him and everyone who lived with him.

It would mean death for me.

So I do not move. I sit instead and force myself to think, remind myself that I know Jerusha wants to leave. What he said about the Minister of Defense does match what I saw in the paper in the train station, the dead body with all the medals, the poem Keran Berj wrote in the Minster's memory.

So Jerusha must know that if he tries to sacrifice me, I will name him.

It is not much safety, but I stay in the seat the soldier told me to because, at least for now, I hold Jerusha's fate in my hands as much as he holds mine in his.

I watch him, though.

I watch him settle into his seat. I watch him turn to the woman who has new, clean clothes on. I watch him smile at her like I didn't know he could, with warm charm, and see the woman smile back. I wonder if Mary smiled at him.

I wonder when she knew she was going to die.

I wonder when she realized she would not be taking Jerusha with her.

CHAPTER 29

Keran Berj had Mary hanged from the largest statue in the City, wrapped a rope around her neck and then made her swing from the statue's head, her face turned so all she could see was Keran Berj's face, his eyes made giant and gleaming gold. It was in the paper for days, brought in by the Rorys when we all came down from the high Hills after that bitter winter.

Mary's things were burned, as was proper, but

no one sang for her. No prayers were offered to make sure the Saints had caught her soul. She had failed and could not be praised. She would never even be mentioned again.

Ann and Lily and I looked through the papers again and again. We wanted to see how she had failed, because Mary was the surest of us all. She had studied so much, and she had been able to walk and talk like she was Keran Berj's flesh and blood better than any of us.

There was nothing about what she did in the papers, though, nothing other than the usual reports of how savage the Angels were, how they and the People killed those who begged for mercy and then danced in their blood, pictures shaping us into twisted, howling monsters.

"Keran Berj is the monster," Ann said, crumpling the paper in one hand. "She must have done something right to get him saying such fierce lies about us all, don't you think?"

"He always lies," Lily said, pointing at the years

of papers we'd had to go through, to learn. "Still, she at least got close enough to Jerusha to make Keran Berj angry. That's something. I would have finished the job, though."

She took the paper from Ann and pointed at the picture, her finger resting on Jerusha's face.

"I would have blotted him out," she told us, and we looked at the photo again.

It was blurry, as if Jerusha was turning away from the camera, but we all knew it was him. He was who Mary was sent for. He would have been there to watch her die.

"I'll do better," Ann said. "I'll break the shackles that bind this land to Keran Berj, I'll—"

She kept talking, but I looked at the picture. At Mary's face, swinging close enough to Keran Berj's gilded one that their lips could have touched.

I thought that if there was a way for Keran Berj to make the statue swallow Mary, he would. He would swallow all of us.

I thought about saying a prayer for her, but I

didn't. She hadn't done anything worth praying for. She'd just died, and my heart only remembered that she'd never wanted to see us as alike. That she'd insisted we weren't. She wanted to show that she was purer of heart and belief than anyone else. She wanted death.

She'd gotten it.

CHAPTER 30

I watch Jerusha now and think of her.

Mary would have killed herself rather than talk to him like I did.

If she was where I am—if she was here, facing what I'm facing—she would try to kill Jerusha again instead of watching him.

But I don't move. I sit. I watch.

She was right. We are not alike at all.

Jerusha gives the girl my tea. I swallow, wishing I had taken it with me, that the coolness she's swallowing was running down my own throat. I run my hands through my hair—still damp, always damp—and then look at my fingers.

It could be the setting sun, but I think there is yet another bit of yellow stained across my skin.

I should have died when I was supposed to. It would not have hurt like this waiting. I would not feel like I do now.

I would not know what it is like to hope.

I would have no idea what that word really means.

It is so hot. The setting sun cuts the train into slices of bright light and brings even more heat, heat that makes my head spin. Makes me want to close my eyes. But I do not want to fall asleep. I will not fall asleep. I want to be awake when the Guards come.

I know I cannot trust anyone but myself, and if

they come for me—and I am so afraid they will—I have to take Jerusha with me. Not for the People. Not for the Saints. Not for Mary. For me.

I watch the sun burn the sky until my vision blurs.

CHAPTER 31

*T*he train stops. I know because I almost fall out of my seat, woken from the cobwebs of a dream about the stage and blood-dead flowers as the train shrieks, shuddering to a halt.

I don't remember falling asleep, but I did.

I did and now it is dark out, stars brilliant against the night sky. The window is cold when I touch my fingers to it, so cold it burns my skin.

The only light I see is the faint, flickering glow of small lamps that some soldiers are carrying. I used to lie on the ground and watch for that very glow. Everyone who lives in the Hills, even Angels, must take their turn at watch.

You must always know when the enemy is coming.

The soldiers are holding a bottle—the bottle of tea I bought earlier—and their lamps spark off it, shedding little rays of light into the dark of the train.

Behind the soldiers are Guards.

Guards standing and watching, waiting, and back behind them I see the glimmer of polished tick-tock shoes, the man from the train station returned. Come all the way out here into the dark of the desert.

There is nothing else to see. We are near nothing. We are nowhere, the perfect place to drag someone off to meet death.

The only reason to be here is death.

I've heard the Guards shoot you in the back of the head if they feel like being kind.

Please let them be kind.

Please.

The soldiers turn back toward the train. The Guards stay behind, waiting, disappearing into the dark. They do not carry lamps.

For what they do, there is no need.

The soldiers come into the train car. They fill it up, their faces grim.

"Who does this belong to?" the soldier who moved me says, yelling so loudly that his voice echoes off the stripped metal of the train.

Silence. Nothing but frozen, scared silence.

And then Jerusha stands up.

"I know who it belongs to," he says, and his voice is clear. His face is calm. Cold.

He can live through anything. He will survive.

He, of all people, might be the one who can destroy Keran Berj.

No wonder he was kept so close.

"Who?" the soldier says, scowling. "You?"

Jerusha sighs, as if he is talking to someone very stupid.

"If it was me, why would I say a word?" he says. "I spoke to you after the last time the train stopped, remember? I asked if my sister could move."

"I remember," the soldier says. "Go on."

"Well, you were by our seats. You saw there was nothing in my hands. Nothing in my seat." He points to the woman sitting next to him. "She got on at the stop, though. She sat down here, and she had a bott—"

He's cut off as the woman starts screaming, shaking her head and saying, "No, no, it was there, it was on the train already, he pulled it out and said—"

The soldier hits her. The woman howls and then falls silent, stunned.

"She did board then, didn't she?" he says to himself, and then looks at the other soldiers, who nod. He turns back to Jerusha. "Did you see her talking to anyone before she boarded?"

"Just a man, an earth-dark man who . . ." Jerusha trails off, then says, "Wait. Is she—does she—is she one of them? Those—those People?" He spits the word as if it is too awful to fit in his mouth, too awful to be said, and stares at the woman in horror.

The soldier pulls the woman up, stares into her crying face. "The Guards contacted us earlier. Told us to look for a woman traveling alone with short, dyed hair. Is that you, do you think?" He yanks her head forward, pulling her hair, and she screams.

He holds up a clump of it. It is white like the brightest sunlight on top and a darker, deeper yellow near the root. Not light brown-red, though.

Not like mine.

"Dyed hair," the soldier says, and the woman cries, "For Keran Berj, for his glory, for how he says women should be," but the soldier shakes her, hard, and says, "We know everything. You asked a soldier to throw the bottle away a little while ago. Off the train, you said, because the trash was full. You think we don't know what you are? You think you didn't give yourself away the moment you showed papers saying you're checking on soil conditions between here and the border? You think that would fool anyone other than some desert rejects?"

"But I am checking on soil conditions and the tea—he gave it to me!" the woman says, pointing at Jerusha.

"Except he didn't have it because I saw him. You were the one who tried to get rid of it."

"No, I just asked a soldier to throw it away because the trash is full, and he said he'd throw it off the train. I didn't ask that. I'm not—my papers are real! I believe in Keran Berj!"

"Of course you do," the soldier says, and then starts to drag her off the train.

She screams, pleading for someone to look at her papers, to call her office.

She is still screaming when the Guards appear again, lit by the soldiers' lamps.

The lamps are switched off and as darkness falls again there's the sound of low voices and her sobbing. It goes on for a moment and then there is silence.

It is so quiet I think the stars will fall from the sky.

But they don't. They stay, shining brightly far away, and the silence on the train is complete, endless.

Eventually, the train begins to move again.

The woman is not on it.

CHAPTER 32

I press my face against the window, feel the bitter cold bite into my skin. I should not be glad I am alive—I know what that woman's fate was— but I am.

I do not move when someone sits next to me. I know who it is.

"You knew this would happen," I say, looking away from the window, looking at him, and Jerusha says, "Yes."

"The man who sold me the water—"

"His hands," Jerusha says. "They were like mine. No marks from labor, no dirt under his nails. He's never touched the ground in his life except to kick people into it."

"But why did you . . . ?" I say, and trail off as I see something in the darkness of the train car, something I couldn't see when I looked at him before because the light only showed me what I knew. It showed me Jerusha, the monster.

I never thought to look past it.

"Mary," I say, surprised, and Jerusha echoes it back, his voice shaking.

In my mind's eye, I see the last picture I saw of him again now. How he was turned so the camera didn't catch him. Turned so he didn't have to see the body swinging from Keran Berj's monument to himself. Turned so he didn't have to see Mary die.

"She should be here," he says.

I don't know what to say. I've seen the mark around his neck. I've seen what she tried to do.

I know she wouldn't want to be here.

"I found out who she was. What she was," he says, and his voice is so thick with something I cannot name that my skin prickles. "And if I knew, Keran would find out. There's no way to keep a secret from him, not ever." He shakes his head. "But I thought I could—I thought maybe I could save her. I thought . . . I thought she'd want to get away. Be . . . be free."

I think of everything I was taught, and I know exactly what she would have said to him when he spoke of being free.

"We—the People—fight for freedom, to live as we will. All else must be set aside for that."

"That's exactly what she said," he says, and I recognize what's in his voice now. Bitterness. "And when I said, 'Freedom depends on setting aside everything in its name,' she smiled at me for real for the first time—the only time—and said, 'Yes, now you see.'"

I stare at him, a chill creeping up my spine. Those words are so similar. The People and Keran Berj and . . . no. I push the thought away. It's not how it sounds.

It can't be.

I can't have been taught what Jerusha was.

I can't.

I swallow. "It's different for us. We mean it."

He looks at me. "And so does Keran Berj every time he says it, which is at the end of almost every speech. So how is it different?"

I look at my hands. I am tired of thinking. Of trying to find the right thing to say when everything I know has a mirror image that I am terrified to see, but do.

"I don't know," I finally say. "I just . . . All I know is that I don't want death anymore."

And there it is. I don't want death. I want life.

The opposite of everything I know. That I was taught to believe. To do.

"Mary did," he says, and I look at him.

"She asked you to—?"

"No," he says. "After I found out who she was, I told her she had to go, that she wasn't safe, but she wouldn't . . ." He stops speaking, and I know he is touching the closed collar of his shirt. Thinking about what lies underneath.

"She cut me along my scar," he says after a moment. "I stood there, blood everywhere, my blood in her hair, on her face, and thought 'If this is what she wants,' but then—" He sighs. "I didn't want to die. I called for help. I told her I lov—I said things to her. And she laughed at me. Said I was nothing. Said that when I died she was going after Keran Berj."

"So you handed her over to him."

"No," he says. "I still wanted to save her. I still thought I could. So I hit her with a sculpture of

Keran Berj, put my Guard sash in her mouth to keep her quiet—I was in training for them, was going to be the Chief Guard one day—and shoved her into my wardrobe. I was going to let her out. I was going to make her leave the City. I didn't think—" I hear him swallow.

"She was found," I say. "And Keran Berj killed her."

"Not him," he says, voice cracking. "I was in the hospital for a week because of the cut. Not that long, but I hadn't told anyone about her being in the house, said I didn't know who'd tried to kill me, that they'd gotten away, and she—she was there in the wardrobe without water. A person can't live—"

"I know," I say, because I do. The Rorys sometimes leave soldiers tied to the ground with their water bottles just out of reach, a message to those that find them.

"Not everyone knows that," he says. "I asked

a girl at a dinner party about it right before . . . right before I left. I said, 'Do you know how long a person can live without water?' and she smiled and shook her head and pressed up against me even though she was shaking with fear. Even though we both knew she didn't want to be near me."

"Because of who you are."

He smiles at me, starlight showing a quick glimpse of teeth, of his mouth curled feral. "Yes," he says. "Because of who I am. What I did. The Minister of Defense wrote a poem celebrating my accomplishments after I got out of the hospital. He read it to me while he had people pull Mary out of the wardrobe. He'd found her there two days before I came home—he didn't believe that I didn't know who'd tried to kill me, and he knew where to look—but he waited until I was there to take her out. The Minister said he knew I'd want to see how I'd managed to kill her."

"And you watched him pull her body out?"

And after that, he'd watched Keran Berj hang her corpse.

"Of course," he says. "I know what happens when you don't obey. You die. I know that better than anyone, don't I?"

CHAPTER 33

I look at him. "Don't you see that's why there has to be change? All Keran Berj brings is death. You know that. You just said so."

"And what will your People do?" he says, staring at me. "What changes will they bring? What did they do to you when you didn't obey? When you didn't die like they wanted?"

"They didn't kill me. And they don't teach children to kill their parents."

"You're right," he says. "They just left you behind instead, made it so your only choice was Christaphor and then me. And of course they teach children to kill others, or kill themselves and others. Isn't that what you learned? What you were?"

Yes.

I sit silently for a moment and then spit out, "Why didn't you do what Mary would have wanted you to?"

He looks away then. "You already know I don't want to die. Isn't that why we're both here?"

"No, not that and you—you know what I mean. Why didn't you kill Keran Berj?"

"I . . . what change would that bring? You think his death would truly make this world different?" He blows out a breath, closing his eyes briefly.

"You tried to do it," I say, shocked. "You did try to do it and you failed, didn't you? That's why you're really here."

"I didn't try to kill Keran Berj," he says, his voice brittle. "I wanted the Minister of Defense to die because he—I wanted him to die, and he did. I got up one night, got out the pistol Keran Berj gave him for his birthday, woke him up, and shot him."

"You . . . you lived with him?"

"He was my guardian." Jerusha says. "He was the one who helped me write what I'd heard my parents say for Keran Berj. He came to their house, ate dinner with them, and then asked if he could take me for a walk. He sat me down on the bench by Keran Berj's statue in Berj Park and said he'd been given my letter. He said he was proud of me, that he could tell I was special, and that he'd help me with my letter, make it better."

"So he—"

"No," Jerusha says. "I wanted to do it. I didn't want to leave home and go somewhere far away. I wanted to stay in school with my friends. I wanted to be like Keran Berj said he was. So I wrote down everything the Minister told me to and when my parents were arrested I stood next to Keran

Berj and told them they were bad for wanting to leave."

He touches my arm and when I flinch, he lets out a little sigh. "That's exactly what Mary did when I told her the story. That's how I knew she came from the People. Every girl Keran sent me had that response trained out of her. He's good at it, wants to keep all their fear for himself. But Mary was— there was still something real about her. Inside her. She believed in things and I . . . I wanted that for myself. Just for a little while."

Like she was a thing. Like she wasn't a person. I wonder if anyone has ever been real to him and a shudder travels across my skin. I don't pull away, though. I just press my feet into the hot floor instead. The pain is familiar now.

"That's how I know you want to live," he says. "She pulled away from me. You don't."

"You want to live too. You didn't die for her, you didn't even do what she would have wanted," I say, hating him for making me sound as weak as I am. Hearing him say what I want sounds so simple, but so selfish. I have turned my back on a lifetime of training, of beliefs everyone around me found easy to carry. I turned to myself and I . . .

I am not sorry for it. Not like I should be.

"Yes, I want to live too," he says, and I hear something strange in his voice, look over and see that the night sky has lightened enough to show his face is tense and sad. "I wrote down what the Minister said I needed to. I didn't cry when Keran Berj told me my parents could never come home because the Minister said not to, and moved into his house after I watched them die because he said he would make sure I never had to leave. He said he would always watch over me because I was so special to him."

He looks at me. "I learned what special meant to him then. Years of it, of being *special*, and then I watched him grin at Mary's body. I told him I was glad he was there when he looked at me. I memorized his poem and recited it to Keran Berj before they hanged her corpse as a warning to the People. I told him I was grateful for everything he'd done to protect me before he fell asleep the night I shot him."

"He—the Minister—?"

"Yes."

"But you are so important to Keran Berj. He wouldn't—"

"You're really surprised, aren't you?" he says, and there is astonishment in his own voice. "You, who claim to know exactly what he is capable of?"

"But you were a child."

"Once," he says, and his voice is thick with a feeling I know, that I've lived with forever. Shame. Shame for having blood in me that made it so I could never truly be one of the People. Shame for being sent to Angel House so Da could prove his worth and be rid of the memory of my mother. Shame that I never believed in what I was taught like I should have. Shame that in spite of all the lessons and prayers that when I thought about forever—about living beyond this world—I didn't want to die.

CHAPTER 34

"You didn't kill the Minister for Mary," I say, thinking of how I took the belt from Liam's hips. How I didn't look for Da. How I pushed the bomb down and walked away from it, far away enough to be safe.

To live.

"No," he says. "It was for me. I did it because I stayed with him for years and never . . . I stayed. I did it because I could have turned away when they arrested my parents, when I realized they were truly going to die, and I didn't. I did it because I watched them hang. Keran Berj would have killed me before their necks even had a chance to snap if I'd only looked away. So I didn't. I wanted to live. I just—no matter what happens, I keep wanting to live. Just like you killed thirty-four people but not who you were supposed to, and not yourself. You weren't thinking about them. You think about you. About surviving. I understand that. I understand you."

Thirty-four people? I killed thirty-four people? "I didn't know—I never thought—"

"About them?" he says, and there is nothing I can say in reply.

Because I didn't think about that. In all the thinking I've done about that day, about the bomb, I never thought about them. About the people who were there.

People who died the day I decided I wanted to live.

Why have I never wondered about them? I've thought about how I could have died, should have died, but I never thought about what happened to the crowd when the bomb went off, never thought about the people around me, in front of me. I never—

I never even looked at them.

I looked at the fire. I've dreamed of the flowers, of blood. Of it all over me, in me until it is all I am.

But it already is.

I am as bad as Jerusha. I am a killer.

And yet he has thought about what he's done while I—

I haven't.

"I didn't think about it at first either," he says, as if he knows my thoughts and he does. He does. "I was six years old, and I just wanted my parents to stop talking about leaving. But once it started, I couldn't stop it, and afterward I just—I had to put it away for a long time. The thing is, the scar—it wasn't from them. They never tried to hurt me. Keran Berj strung me up on a rope in front of them until they confessed."

He rubs his shirt collar, touching that top button once again. "They did it right away, but he left me there, made them watch me struggle. He asked me if I understood why he was doing it and I said I did. I just wanted the pain to stop and when it did I didn't . . . I didn't even look at my parents when he cut me down and told me to go. I just left. I never even told them goodbye."

"Do you . . . do you think about them now?"

"Yes," he says, a simple, broken word.

I look out the window. The stars are fading, drifting away as the dark sky slowly fills with morning light.

I take a deep breath.

CHAPTER 35

*T*hey'll forgive you," I say slowly, hating the words as I say them but knowing they're true. "Over the border, I mean. Everyone will forgive you for what happened. You were young. You—you got broken by terrible things. And now you have a way to stop Keran Berj. You have those codes you took. You'll be a hero. The past will . . . it will be understood. Forgotten."

Jerusha laughs, softly. "I'll remember though,

won't I? And I only took the codes because I knew it would frighten him. No other reason, no grand plans. I've been a hero, and I have enough blood on my hands for a lifetime from it. I don't—I don't want to stand for anything to anyone again. Not ever."

"But you have to stop—"

"That's the thing," he says. "I don't have to do anything. I don't have to live for others. I can live for myself, and that's what I want. That's my freedom."

I don't want to understand, but I do.

I understand him.

Jerusha wants what I do, and we both chose to be on this train, with all the risks it carries—risks I've now seen so closely.

We have both chosen life—and ourselves—over what we had.

We have chosen ourselves over death.

I always knew it was coming for me, but it would have come for Jerusha too. He knows Keran

Berj's world better than I ever could, and even I know that those Keran Berj trusts most, "loves" most, always die.

So now we are here, on this train, waiting for the final stop to come. Behind us, we have left a trail. One of bodies. Victims.

We are both running from what we were, from what we did and did not do.

"You'll have what you want," I whisper. "You'll be free, finally."

He touches the collar of his shirt and then looks at me. "You understand. You really do. No one else ever—" He breaks off, looking out the window, but I know he doesn't see what is going by. He is seeing the past. Before. Keran Berj. The Minster of Defense. Mary.

"That's why I made you move," he says after a moment. "It's why I . . . it is why I said what I did when the Guards came. You were supposed to be taken. Christaphor sent you so you could—"

"Be caught," I say, thinking of how simple

things would have been for Jerusha if that had happened. "I was sent to be caught so you could escape. Chris knew no one from the People would ever travel willingly with Jerusha. He thought I would—"

"Yes," he says. "He told me you'd be obvious, that you were a Hill girl, and that when you realized who I was you'd do anything to get away from me. You'd expose yourself, leaving me safe. But you weren't obvious. And you were willing to travel with me after you knew who I was. I wasn't sure until . . . " He trails off, and I know both of us are thinking of things we've done on the train. Of how we've kept going afterward.

Of how we've kept going our whole lives.

Of how now we are on this train. How the ride we've taken, the one I've sweated through, worried through, and discovered things through, is almost over.

I am hopeful in a way I have never been before.

I am terrified too. That emotion is so much more familiar to me.

I have spent my whole life waiting to die. Not wanting to, but waiting.

I saw the difference the day I walked away, and this train ride has taught me I will do anything to survive. I will even sit next to Jerusha.

And I am not, and will not ever be, sorry that I am.

GRACE

CHAPTER 36

I want to live as I choose," I say to him, and the truth is bitter on my tongue, in my heart. But it is the truth, and I've known it since I looked up at that cloudless blue sky and realized I didn't want to be in it.

I don't mind telling him this. He has seen what I will do to live.

We have both seen what each other will do to survive, and it is because of him I am here now.

He is not . . . he is everything and yet nothing like I thought he was.

"I do too," Jerusha says, and he truly is Kerr, who wants to escape as much as I do. He is the person who came to me in the train station what feels like a lifetime ago. But he is also someone else. He carries a past that will always be with him. "It's a strange thing to want. A shameful thing. But I still want it. I have for a long time."

Now I look out the window, thinking about what he has said. Off in the distance, in the faint yellow light that signals day has truly begun, I can just make out the border. I can see the crossing and the Guard Station we will have to pass through to reach it.

The Guard Station looks like a simple building, but my heart beats fast and hard. I have waited to see this. I have longed to see this, and it is everything and nothing like I thought it would be.

Just like Jerusha.

I know that past the border gate is a long, stone

walkway. I know that after I cross it, I will be in a place where Keran Berj does not rule. I will be in a place where his words are just words.

I will be in a place where there are no Hills. No People.

I will be in a place where I can be Grace, just Grace, and I want that. I want that more than I have ever wanted anything.

I cannot see the shame in that.

"Why is it shameful?" I whisper, turning away from the window, and he looks at me, startled.

"I don't know," he says slowly. "It just is."

"Yes," I say softly, as I remember what I spent a lifetime learning. As I remember all we have both done to be here.

We stare at each other.

I know exactly what he is thinking because I am thinking it too.

It should be shameful. We were both taught that it was. That it is.

And we both believed it, but now—

Now neither of us do because life shouldn't be something you want to hide. It shouldn't be something you turn away from.

Will we be able to embrace it like we want?

Can we?

I don't know. I just know that I want to, and that Jerusha does too.

Mary didn't.

Mary was who I was supposed to be. Mary was an Angel.

Mary believed.

Mary thought her life meant death and never once questioned that. She wasn't and didn't and never would have lived for anyone at all.

She believed, and that is why Jerusha loved her.

CHAPTER 37

*H*e hasn't said so, although I heard enough of
the word when he spoke of her to know it is how
he felt.

But he doesn't have to say it. I understand why
he loved her.

She believed and that was what caught him. Belief was something he'd once had, even though it
was in a very different form.

Mary was who Jerusha wanted to be, but wasn't

anymore. She was who he could never be again.

She was a reminder of who he was when life was simple. When it was just about belief, and that was all he'd needed.

I'd never had Mary's belief. I had resented her for so much, for nearly everything she did. But the thing I hated most was how she accepted it all.

She never wondered like I did. It was so easy for her to believe that her death would bring not just the People, but her, glory.

How could she have believed that? Without hesitation. Without question.

I don't know, but I do know why Jerusha loved her.

Mary was so sure of why she was here. She never once thought something like "Why?" She never, ever would have.

But I did, and he did too.

Jerusha and I wondered, and so now we are both sitting on this train, alive and waiting for it to make its last stop. The final one.

Can this really be it? Am I really near the end of this long, strange, and surprising trip?

I am sitting here, sweating, hoping, and afraid.

I am sitting here with someone I always saw as Death by my side.

Is this what I left everything for? Is this worth it?

Yes.

I look around the train slowly, cautiously, and for the first time, I truly notice who else is in the car with us. I see they aren't just sheep. They are people, and they are as real as I am. As Jerusha is.

And all of them look tired, look anxious. All of them know the world we live in.

They all have their reasons for being on this train, and for the first time I wonder what they are all doing here. If any of them think like I do. Like Jerusha does.

I wonder if any of the People ask themselves the questions I did and do. I wonder if any of Keran

Berj's followers did or do too. I know that some-where; in the City, in the desert, or even in the Hills, I am not alone.

There are those who wonder like I did and do. Like Jerusha did and does. We cannot be the only people who have looked at death and realized it isn't life at all.

I think again of the people who were there when I chose life. I think of the people I killed. I don't know if they ever wanted what I did, but I took everything from them.

I took what I am afraid of losing. I took what sent me running to Chris, to the train.

I took what sent me here, to now.

I took life when I chose my own.

I can see the final stop more clearly now, and the train begins to slow down.

CHAPTER 38

*A*s the train brakes, wheezing with effort, the people around us begin to straighten up. They comb their hair or pluck at their clothes, trying to pull out wrinkles. They all look out the window.

They all pull out their papers, getting ready to go as far as Keran Berj's leash will allow.

Jerusha leans over and scratches his ankle, then pulls out a folded stack of bills. He sees me look-

ing at them and says, "You have to pay a fee before you can cross. Christaphor didn't tell you that,
did he?"

"No," I say, thinking of Chris handing me coins
and shoving me into the night. I think of the last
bit of money I had. How I used it to buy tea that
could have cost me my life. Should have.

"I have enough for two," he says, and when I
look at him he smiles—a strange, hesitant thing.
A real smile. "I told him I had no money and took
everything he gave me, then added it to what I
already had. I told him I'd never say a word to you
about it. I told him I understood why he'd kept
you alive, what you were for. But I'm tired of how
death is supposed to mean nothing to me. It isn't
like that. It—"

"It marks you," I say, thinking that if I'd done
what I'd been told to that day in the village, I
would be a hero to the People. I would be beyond
this world; I wouldn't have to live with the deaths

I created. The deaths I never thought about until Jerusha made me see what I'd done.

I will never be able to look at flowers again. I looked at them that day and saw their death, felt for the earth, but I never thought about who held those flowers. I never wondered what happened to those little girls. There are thirty-four people I tore out of this world. I never once thought of them, and now there are thirty-four people I must carry with me. That I cannot forget.

That I will not forget because they are marked inside me. Their blood is on my hands and in my heart.

In the end, I created death just like I was supposed to.

I wish I hadn't.

Life was simpler before Jerusha opened my eyes. It was simpler when I didn't know him, when he was Death and nothing more.

His hands are bloody too. I will never forget

that. But I also know he will not forget either. I see the price he paid for that blood, and it was not the nothing I believed it was. All his choices were shaped by Keran Berj.

Keran Berj created him for a reason, and I believed in that creation.

He was Keran Berj's creature, but what grew in Jerusha's heart was something else. Something that wanted more.

He is as much a person as I am. He even loved.

He loved Mary, who didn't love him back. Who was a reminder of everything from when his life was simple. But it was still love.

I have never loved anyone like that.

I have never loved anyone besides myself. It gave me the strength to get here, but what it cost . . . I do not know what it will cost me.

I do know what I will have to remember forever. Who I will have to remember. How I never once thought to look back in the village. I never once thought to see if anyone was hurt as I chose to walk away. As I chose life.

. I fold my hands together, and after a moment Jerusha touches my shoulder clumsily. Kindly. I do not flinch away, but I want to. I just don't know if it is from him or myself.

We sit in silence until the train stops. No one moves for a long time, but then the doors finally creak open, the soldiers leaving first, stepping off into the sunlight that's rapidly filling the sky.

CHAPTER 39

Jerusha and I do not get off right away. We both sit, watching others go. From our car, from others, they venture out slowly. Some are old and some are young. Some are clearly in a hurry, and some are hanging back a little, smoothing their clothes or hair again. Looking at their papers again.

I wonder what they will all do when they cross the border. Will they think of the train? Will they be eager to go back? Will they think of their lives with pleasure? Can they?

I have never known pleasure with the People. I did love the Hills, but I was able to leave them behind.

I left them because all they are is a place where people are born to die.

I think of the City, of the people I saw waiting in lines. Of the tick-tock man, and the terror he brought. That was Jerusha's world, and he left it for the same reasons I left mine.

Keran Berj's world and the People's world, the worlds Jerusha and I have traveled through, are ones that promise that death brings glory. That life is only about death.

But it shouldn't be.

Life is about being alive. It is about *living*.

If that choice—life—has made us both do things that have stained our minds and souls, it is a price I am willing to pay. I will pay in memory.

I will pay by standing by my choice to be here. To be alive.

I will leave the beliefs I was told were true behind. I will find ones that will show me how to hold life gently. That will teach me to respect others and not see them as less than human.

Jerusha already knows these things, and yet he let me judge him. He let me judge him, and he saved me. He is actually more human than I am.

He is more human than anyone I have ever known.

And he is so alone. I have never had a friend, not a true one, but at least I had the Hills, the land, around me. He only had Keran Berj.

Jerusha has never had anything or anyone to really depend on since he was very young. He has never had a true friend.

We have both traveled down strange roads, down paths full of lies. Jerusha saw the evil in his, and I saw the empty heart of mine.

We have both done terrible things to be here.

We have both come so far to be new. I know we will both try to do that now. Not just because we want to live, but also because we have to.

We must live to remember what we have done.

We will get off this train and try to cross the border.

We may not make it across. I know that. I have always known that, and I know he does too.

And so Jerusha and I wait, only leaving when the flow of people exiting the train has slowed to a trickle. We can see people walking toward the Guard Station and the border. Toward the path that curves off into the distance.

My feet don't hurt anymore. I am ready to stand.

I am lighter than air, soaring.

CHAPTER 40

*A*s Jerusha and I get off the train, every breath I take tastes like a beginning, and the sun is beautiful, gilding everything and everyone around us.

I have never felt so alive. I ache, I am exhausted, but I am here at the border.

And I am here because I was helped by someone I was taught to hate.

Jerusha has helped me, but more than that, he has shown me something. I see that everyone around us is not a thing. Not a sheep. I see that everyone is a person.

Everyone I see matters to someone else.

Everyone who has died by my hand or at the whim of Keran Berj or from the People's fury is mourned.

It is not just one person, or even one group of people who matter, who deserve to live.

I see that now. Everyone deserves life. It has taken me so long to reach this point.

It has taken me my whole life.

And now here I stand where I have struggled to be. Where I have longed to be.

Here I am, and I am scared.

I see the border, marked by a thin line painted on rocks resting on the sand. I see the station we must pass through to reach it. I see the path that lies just beyond it.

I see Guards standing by it, waiting. Their faces are a blur in the morning light.

Jerusha stands still beside me. He knows as well as I do what could happen now.

I tense, then hold out my hand like a sister would.

Like a friend would.

After a moment, Jerusha clasps his hand to mine.

I let my fingers twine with his, and we walk together into the light. To the waiting path. To the border.

To life.

Acknowledgments

*M*any thanks to Julie Strauss-Gabel, who looked at this book, saw what it could be, and made it all happen.

Thanks also go to Lisa Yoskowitz, for always being so kind to me.

As always, thanks to the usual suspects, including everyone who read drafts of this book, especially Jessica Brearton, Katharine Beutner, Clara Jaeckel, and my husband.

And of course, thanks go to Robin Rue, who always believes in me, and to Diana Fox, who has held my hand so many times that I owe her about twenty dinners.

Finally, many, many thanks to The Sheep Meadow Press for permission to use an excerpt from Miklós Radnóti's stunning poem, "Forced March." The poem can be found in *Clouded Sky: Poems by Miklós Radnóti,* with translations by Steven Polgar, Stephen Berg, and S. J. Marks.

TURN THE PAGE
FOR A BONUS CHAPTER OF

GRACE

but you start again   as if you had wings.

The Minister of Culture is tired. He has been traveling for ten days now, ten days of standing and sitting and smiling and sweating as he visits one dusty, hot village after the other.

He liked it so much better when he was Undersecretary to the Minister of Culture, when his job was to fill out forms and send them along, to make sure the Minister had his schedule and knew when he would be traveling.

He was always traveling.

He had envied the Minister for being invited to one of Keran Berj's dinners, though. He had never been, of course, but heard the food was like something out of a dream.

He has been to one of those dinners now, and the food is wonderful, better than a dream because it is real. But there was and is a price to pay for being at Keran Berj's table. For being one of his Ministers.

The last Minister of Culture paid with his life. Keran Berj had turned to him after the hanging and said, "I know you'll do a better job. You look like a good man."

The Minister's wife used to say that. She does not anymore, but then he cannot blame her. She does not like being followed, although she knows well enough not to say anything about that. She simply goes and waits in lines like she always has, spends her days gathering what she can, and ignores the presents of food that arrive from time to time.

The Minister opens them, as he must, and eats the food in the office where everyone can see. He smacks his lips and smiles even as his stomach churns.

He has not been a good man for a long time.

This village is the same as all the others, small and primitive. Last night he slept on a pile of rugs by an open window and longed for his bed, for the small sounds his wife makes when she is sleeping.

Sometimes he will touch her hair, the only comfort he dares allow himself to have. Tonight he fears he will be kept awake by villagers eager to tell him how Keran Berj has made their lives better.

He will listen and wonder if he sounds like them when he talks about his own life.

He will know he does.

But for now he just has to make his speech. The reading of the missives is almost finished, and the Minister hopes the Festival of Glorious Freedom has not yet been changed to something else. It is hard to get messages from his office so far from the City, and he worries he will miss something.

He knows the price he will pay if he does.

There, the missives are done, and now the request for money is being read. The Minister wonders what Keran Berj will do with his ice palace when it is built. He suspects it will sit there in the desert, unseen and glorious-looking.

The Minister had a daughter, once. She was twelve when she whispered to a friend that if one of Keran Berj's statues was melted down, she was sure there would be enough gold for every girl in the City to have at least two pairs of earrings all her own.

He and his wife removed every picture they had of her as soon as she was arrested. They do not speak of her.

On the anniversary of her death, they make sure they are seen out and about together, smiling and carefree.

His wife will not cry. She is afraid someone will hear.

The Minister does cry, though. Every year, after the long day that marks the moment when his daughter's life ended, he cries silently before he pretends to fall asleep, sobs that don't even shake the bed, that his wife closes her eyes and heart to.

And now it is finally time for his speech. He stands up slowly. The stage seems so far away, and the steps so very high. He makes it up them carefully, sweating and tired. The people are looking at him as they always do, and as he starts to clear his throat to begin, three little girls come on stage, their arms full of flowers.

They are so young and so happy to be on stage, to be the center of attention. He smiles at the sight of their happy innocence, and hopes it never changes for them, that these girls stay here, in this hot and dusty village, and live long, dull, and safe lives.

One of the little girls waves at her parents, and the flowers in her arms dip, trembling.

People clap, and the Minister wishes he didn't have to speak at all. He wishes that this village's one moment of happiness could be all that is needed. That he could just leave and go home.

But of course that can't happen. The applause changes, turns more polite, turns toward him, and now everyone is looking at him, everyone is waiting for him to speak. Everyone is waiting to hear what Keran Berj wants them to do.

I'm sorry.

That's what he wants to say.

He will never say that, though. He watched his daughter die. He cannot bear the thought of having to watch his wife die as well, and knows that would happen if and when his time comes. He does not want to lose the only person left whom he loves and who once loved him, even if it was long ago.

He opens his mouth, but nothing comes out. Instead, the entire world goes white. Not a soft, gentle white, but a harsh one, white-hot and burning.

He lets it carry him away, prays it takes him out of this world, and his last thought is: *Angel.*

They are supposed to be cruel, but this—this is a kindness.

When he wakes up in the City hospital, he starts to cry. He says it is because he is so happy he is alive.

He lies.

QUESTIONS FOR DISCUSSION

- What forms does freedom take in this novel? What does it mean to be free in this story? What does freedom mean to you?

- Do you think Grace is cowardly or brave in her decisions?

- Grace doesn't approve of her fellow Angel, Mary's, idea of freedom. Can freedom ever be a bad thing?

- What is the role of fear in this novel? How do you think fear motivates different characters in the story?

- Jerusha points out that both the People and Keran Berj's followers kill others, so they aren't so different from one another. Do you think this is true? Why or why not? Do you think one group is better than the other?

- Grace mentions Liam a lot, even though he was only in her life for a short time. Why? In what ways did he impact her life?

- The Rorys and the Guards both want control of the Hills. What do you think the Hills symbolize?

- How does nature mirror the plot of this novel? In what ways do the desert, the sky, and the sun help us to understand Grace's internal state?

- Jerusha and Grace do everything—including committing acts of violence—in order to survive. Do you think this makes their acts justified?

- "Choice" is an important theme in this novel. What choices do you feel that Grace has in the story? What things does she not have a choice about?

- Jerusha and Grace come from opposite sides of the war in their country. What do you think draws them together?

- Grace writes about Mary, "She believed, and that is why Jerusha loved her" (page 184). What do you think she means by this?

- Why do you think this story is mostly set on a train? How is setting important to this novel?

- How do Grace's views on life and death change throughout the story? Has the story affected your views as well?

- What are the consequences of choosing life in this novel? Are they different if you choose death?

TURN THE PAGE FOR A PEEK AT
ELIZABETH SCOTT'S NEXT NOVEL,

1.

WAKE UP.

I'm in bed. Sheets and blankets tucked around me, my legs sprawled out like I've fallen. No light in the room except faint yellow and a darker, colder gleam shining through the window, its curtains only partly closed.

Where am I?

I don't know these sheets, this bed, this room.

I look down at myself, see soft fabric wrapping me from neck to knees. My feet are bare.

There are dark shapes all around.

People?

I slide up onto my elbows slowly, creeping back until my shoulders hit the wooden back of the bed. I sit quiet, watching. Waiting.

No movement. No breathing other than my own.

There are no people here, just things. Chair. Dresser. Desk. Lamp. I can see them as my eyes adjust to the dark. Familiar shapes, words easy on my tongue but still—

I don't recognize these dark shapes, these things.

Where am I?

I get up.

The door to the room I'm in opens easily, unlocked, swinging free, and I step into a hall. It's dark and there is carpet under my feet, thick and soft. It extends out past me, leads to two closed doors.

What hides behind them?

I don't want to look.

Stairs. I see them now, a little to my left, and move toward them, grateful. I do not know where they lead, but it has to be away and that—that is better than those closed doors.

The stairs are carpeted too, soft under my feet, and down and down and down I walk into more darkness.

I can walk. I can talk, whisper "carpet" into the dark. I know words: hands, door, nightgown, bed, dark, light.

Where am I?

Bottom of the stairs, wood under my feet now, I'm standing on a floor, darkness all around edged only by the deeper darkness of more rooms, waiting shadows.

Door to my left, just a few steps away.

I move toward it carefully, my feet silently crossing

the floor. I see my toes, but they do not feel like mine. I am dreaming maybe, one where everything is familiar but not, understood but not known.

I open the door.

Night, it is night, and a streetlight glows strong enough that it bleeds across the faint light of stars that strain above it.

Close my eyes.

I think about stars. Their light comes from years beyond years away. Constellations: Big Dipper, Orion. Venus sometimes shines brightly, low in the night sky, and is mistaken for a star.

I open my eyes.

I still don't know here. Don't know this place.

Where am I?

There are more stairs, rugged for outside, for weather, and I walk down them. I walk away from the room, the hall, the stairs.

I turn around, see a tall shape, boxy dark in the night.

A house.

I don't know it.

Where am I?

I back away, step onto grass. It's cold and wet

against my feet, sends a chill crawling through my toes and up my spine.

Walking, I am walking, almost running, off the grass and onto a road, the streetlight beaming at the end of it, glowing over a sign. Homeway Lane.

Where am I?

Street, alley, driveway, walk, road, I know.

I don't know Homeway Lane.

Where am I?

Close my eyes, this is just a dream, a weird, bad dream, like—

I don't know.

I don't know any of my bad dreams. I don't know—

I open my eyes.

It's still dark, still night, my skin is cold and I have goose bumps, but this isn't real, it's just a dream, a bad dream, and I know that just like I know that I am—I am—I am—

I don't know.

I don't know.

Close eyes, shaking now. End dream.